MW00932300

Spike

Dave Sargent

ALL CAPS EDITION

OZARK PUBLICATIONS INC.
439 RHOADS RD.
REDFIELD, AR 72132

i

F
SAR   SARGENT, DAVE
            SPIKE.   OZARK PUBLICATIONS, 1991.
            VI, 174P.
            SUMMARY: SPIKE, A BLACK WOLF, IS
        RAISED BY A YOUNG BOY AND HIS FAMILY. HE
        BECAME A HERO AND A LEGEND AND WAS
        LOVED TO THE END.
            1. WOLVES-FICTION. I. TITLE.

ISBN-0-973-00523-4 HARD BACK
ISBN-1-56763-028-6 PAPER BACK

LIBRARY OF CONGRESS CATALOGUE NUMBER 03-305-704

OZARK PUBLICATIONS INC.
439 RHOADS RD.
REDFIELD, AR 72132
PHO: 1-800-321-5671

FIRST PRINTING 1991
SECOND PRINTING 1993

PRINTED IN THE UNITED STATES OF AMERICA

INSPIRED BY

WHEN I WAS NINE YEARS OLD, I WAS WALKING DOWN AN OLD LOGGING ROAD LOOKING FOR ARROWHEADS. I ROUNDED A BEND IN THE ROAD, LOOKED UP, AND THERE IN FRONT OF ME, NOT TWENTY FEET AWAY WAS A BLACK WOLF. I SCREAMED, THEN TURNED AND RAN AS HARD AS I COULD!

AFTER A TIME, I GLANCED OVER MY SHOULDER TO SEE HOW CLOSE THE WOLF WAS. IT WASN'T FOLLOWING ME. AS A MATTER OF FACT, I HAD PROBABLY SCARED THE WOLF AS MUCH OR MORE THAT IT HAD SCARED ME.

I'VE NEVER FORGOTTEN THAT EXPERI-ENCE. IT WAS THAT EXPERIENCE THAT IN-SPIRED ME TO WRITE THIS BOOK.

DEDICATED

WITH LOVE AND PRIDE
TO MY GRANDDAUGHTERS
AMBER, APRIL AND ASHLEY

Foreword

THIS IS A STORY ABOUT A BLACK WOLF WHO WAS RAISED BY A YOUNG BOY. THE WOLF, AT MATURITY, WAS TORN BETWEEN LOYALTY TO THE ONLY FAMILY SHE HAD EVER KNOWN AND THE CALL OF THE WILD.

THE CALL OF THE WILD WON OUT, BUT SHE CAME BACK ONE DAY AND LEFT ONE OF HER PUPS; A SOLID BLACK MALE. THE LITTLE WOLF PUP WAS NAMED SPIKE. HE WAS A LOYAL AND FAITHFUL COMPANION TO THE BOY AND HIS FAMILY.

SPIKE BECAME A HERO AND A LEGEND AND WAS LOVED TO THE END.

CONTENTS

One

Lucky

We were at the table eating breakfast, when all of a sudden, the horses started whinnying real loud and the chickens started raising a ruckus. I said, "Sally, it sounds like a fox is after the chickens!" I grabbed my rifle and ran outside.

There was a wolf running into the woods, south of the chicken coop. It was solid black. It had one of the chickens in its mouth. I raised my gun to shoot, but it was too late; the wolf was already in the woods. I turned and went back into the house and said, "Sally, we're going to have to get a dog to keep the wolves and foxes scared away."

She said, "I agree. We can't afford to lose any more chickens!"

After finishing breakfast, I went to the barn to check on Bell. She was due to calve any day. Rose was still giving a little milk, but she would need to be dried in about two weeks. I milked Rose, and since it didn't look like Bell would calve for a spell, I let them both out of the barn to drink from the stream and pick at the roughage.

1

I LEFT THE HORSES IN THE BARN BECAUSE I WAS GOING TO START BREAKING GROUND TODAY TO PLANT SPRING OATS AND I WOULD NEED THEM.

I TOOK THE MILK TO THE HOUSE AND SET IT ON THE CABINET FOR SALLY. I HARNESSED THE TEAM AND STARTED PLOWING THE SOUTH FIELD. FOR FEBRUARY, THE WEATHER WAS NICE. IT WAS WARM AND THE GROUND HAD JUST THE RIGHT AMOUNT OF MOISTURE FOR TURNING.

AT NOON, I STOPPED FOR DINNER. I GAVE THE HORSES A SCOOP OF OATS AND SOME HAY. AFTER DINNER AND A SHORT REST, IT WAS BACK TO THE FIELD. IT WAS LATE AFTERNOON BEFORE I CALLED IT A DAY. I UNHARNESSED THE HORSES AND PUT THEM IN THE CORRAL.

I KNEW I'D HAVE TO HURRY THROUGH THE CHORES TO GET FINISHED BEFORE DARK. I STOOD IN FRONT OF THE BARN AND CALLED THE COWS, AND WHILE I WAS WAITING FOR THEM TO COME UP, I FED THE PIGS AND GATHERED THE EGGS.

I TOOK THE EGGS TO THE HOUSE AND GOT THE MILK BUCKET. WHEN I GOT BACK TO THE BARN, ROSE WAS WAITING AT THE DOOR. I LOOKED AROUND AND BELL WASN'T ANY WHERE IN SIGHT. I KNEW I'D BETTER FIND HER BECAUSE SHE WAS DUE TO CALVE; AND IF SHE CALVED OUT IN THE WOODS, THE WOLF WOULD GET THE CALF, FOR SURE. I WENT TO THE STREAM WHERE I HAD LAST SEEN THE COWS AND STARTED CALLING BELL. SHE HAD A SMALL BELL STRAPPED AROUND HER NECK, AND I KNEW I COULD HEAR HER WHEN I GOT CLOSE ENOUGH. I'D WALKED DOWN THE STREAM

OR ABOUT A QUARTER OF A MILE WHEN I BEGAN TO HEAR A FAINT TINKLING SOUND. I STOPPED AND LISTENED. THERE IT WAS AGAIN; I COULD HEAR HER BELL, AND IT SOUNDED LIKE SHE WAS DUE EAST.

AS I HEADED EAST, I COULD TELL THE SOUND OF THE BELL WAS GETTING LOUDER. THE SUN WAS ALREADY DOWN, BUT I KNEW I COULD GET OLD BELL BACK TO THE BARN BEFORE DARK. I KNEW SHE WAS GOING TO CALVE OR SHE WOULDN'T BE THIS FAR FROM THE BARN.

WHEN I FOUND HER, I SAW THAT SHE HAD ALREADY CALVED, AND SOMETHING HAD EATEN MOST OF THE CALF. THERE WAS ONLY A PIECE OF A LEG LEFT!

I FIGURED IT WAS THAT BLACK WOLF! WE COULDN'T AFFORD TO LOSE THAT CALF. WE DEPENDED ON THE CALVES FOR OUR WINTER MEAT. WHAT WITH JAKE GETTING OLDER AND ANOTHER BABY THIS FALL, LOSING THAT CALF WOULD REALLY HURT!

I DROVE BELL BACK TO THE BARN. SHE KEPT TRYING TO GET AROUND ME AND GO BACK TO WHERE HER BABY HAD BEEN BORN, BUT I MANAGED TO KEEP HER GOING. AFTER I GOT HER TO THE BARN, I MILKED ROSE AND WENT TO THE HOUSE AND TOLD SALLY WHAT HAD HAPPENED. SHE WAS UPSET! SHE KNEW HOW IMPORTANT THE CALF WAS TO US.

THE NEXT MORNING, I TOLD SALLY, "I'M GOING TO TRAP THAT BLACK WOLF! WE CAN'T AFFORD TO LOSE ANYTHING ELSE TO THAT BLACK DEVIL!"

SHE SAID, "I HOPE YOU CATCH IT SOON!"

AFTER CHORIN', I GOT ALL MY BIG TRAPS AND

PUT THEM IN THE WASH KETTLE. I FILLED IT HALF FULL OF WATER, THEN BUILT A BIG FIRE UNDER IT AND BOILED THE TRAPS TO GET RID OF THE HUMAN SCENT. AFTER I BOILED THE TRAPS, I COVERED MY HANDS AND SHOES WITH LARD, SO I WOULDN'T LEAVE ANY SCENT ON WHAT I TOUCHED OR STEPPED ON.

I WENT TO THE PORCH AND HOLLERED AT SALLY. WHEN SHE CAME TO THE DOOR, I SAID, "WE'LL HAVE TO SACRIFICE A COUPLE OF CHICKENS TO USE FOR BAIT TO CATCH THE WOLF."

SHE SAID, "THAT'S OK. IT'D BE BETTER TO SACRIFICE A COUPLE THAN TO LOSE THEM ALL."

I TOOK TWO OF THE CHICKENS AND TIED THEM TO LOW-HANGING LIMBS IN TWO DIFFERENT PLACES. I PUT ONE NEAR WHERE BELL HAD HER CALF AND PUT THE OTHER ONE BACK IN THE WOODS WHERE I'D SEEN THE BLACK WOLF. I PLACED THREE STEEL TRAPS AT EACH PLACE, TYING THE TRAPS TO A TREE SO THE WOLF COULDN'T RUN OFF WITH THEM. I COVERED THEM WITH LEAVES. I KNEW THE WOLF WOULD SMELL THE FRESH MEAT, AND WHEN IT CAME IN FOR IT, IT'D GET CAUGHT IN ONE OF THE TRAPS. IT WAS LATE AFTERNOON WHEN I GOT THROUGH. I KNEW IF I CAUGHT THE WOLF, IT MIGHT TAKE TILL MORNING.

EARLY THE NEXT MORNING, AT FIRST LIGHT, I GOT MY GUN AND HEADED OUT TO CHECK THE TRAPS. SURE NUF, CLOSE TO WHERE BELL HAD CALVED, I HAD CAUGHT THE BLACK WOLF! WHEN IT SAW ME, IT CROUCHED AND STARTED SHOWING ITS TEETH! IT WAS STRUGGLING, TRYING TO GET FREE OF THE TRAP! I

4

WAS AFRAID TO GET TOO CLOSE. I KNEW THAT IF THE WOLF DID GET LOOSE, IT WOULD ATTACK ME! I SHOT IT THREE TIMES BEFORE IT FELL.

I APPROACHED THE WOLF WITH CAUTION. WHEN I GOT CLOSE ENOUGH TO SEE IT GOOD, I COULD TELL THAT THE WOLF WAS DEAD. IT WAS A BITCH, AND SHE WAS SOLID BLACK! I COULD TELL SHE WAS FULL OF MILK AND HEAVY WITH PUPS, AND I FIGURED THEY COULD HAVE BEEN BORN ABOUT ANY TIME.

I HAD ALWAYS HEARD THAT WOLVES MAKE GOOD PETS AND ARE VERY PROTECTIVE, SO I DECIDED TO CUT HER OPEN AND SEE IF THE PUPS WERE STILL ALIVE. I THOUGHT IF THEY WERE, I'D TAKE ONE TO JAKE. IT'D SURE MAKE A GOOD PET.

I GOT MY KNIFE OUT AND CUT HER OPEN. I COULD SEE THE PUPS. AS I PULLED THEM OUT, ONE BY ONE, THEY LAY THERE LIFELESS. I WAS TOO LATE; THEY WERE ALREADY DEAD.

WHEN I PULLED OUT THE LAST ONE, ONE OF ITS FEET MOVED; IT WAS STILL ALIVE! I LOOKED AT IT CLOSELY AND SAW THAT IT WASN'T BREATHING, SO I GRABBED A SMALL, DRY TWIG AND STUCK IT IN ITS NOSE TO MAKE IT SNEEZE; IT STARTED BREATHING! I DRIED IT OFF GOOD WITH LEAVES, THEN PUT IT INSIDE MY COAT AND HEADED HOME.

WHEN I GOT TO THE CABIN, I TOOK THE WOLF PUP FROM UNDER MY COAT AND SHOWED IT TO SALLY. SHE SAID, "WHERE DID YOU GET THAT PUPPY? DON'T YOU THINK IT'S A LITTLE TOO YOUNG TO TAKE FROM ITS MOTHER? HOW DO YOU EXPECT TO RAISE ONE THAT

YOUNG?" HER QUESTIONS WERE COMING SO FAST, I DIDN'T HAVE A CHANCE TO ANSWER ANY OF THEM.

I FINALLY SAID, "WHOA, THERE! JUST LISTEN FOR A SECOND AND LET ME TELL YOU WHERE THIS PUP CAME FROM." THEN I TOLD HER ABOUT KILLING THE BLACK WOLF AND GETTING THE PUP.

"I'M GLAD YOU KILLED THE WOLF," SHE SAID, "BUT I'M AFRAID THAT WHEN THAT PUP GETS OLDER, IT'LL TURN ON JAKE OR THE BABY AT ANY TIME!"

I SAID, "I'VE ALWAYS HEARD THAT WOLVES MAKE GOOD PETS AND ARE VERY PROTECTIVE."

SHE SAID, "I DON'T CARE HOW GOOD A PET THEY MAKE, DAVE! I WANT YOU TO TAKE THAT PUP OUT AND DROWN IT!"

I PUT THE PUP UNDER MY COAT AND WENT OUT-SIDE, THEN HEADED TOWARD THE STREAM. WHEN I GOT THERE, I TOOK THE PUP FROM UNDER MY COAT, AND AS I LOOKED AT HER, I REMEMBERED WHAT I'D HAD TO DO TO GET HER TO START BREATHING, AND I JUST COULD-N'T DROWN HER.

SALLY HAD GOTTEN SO MAD ABOUT THE PUP! SHE HAD NEVER BEEN SO INSISTENT ABOUT ANYTHING SINCE WE'D BEEN MARRIED. I KNEW I COULDN'T TAKE IT BACK TO THE HOUSE; I ALSO KNEW I COULDN'T KILL IT. I FINALLY DECIDED TO PUT IT IN THE BARN. THE FEED BOX WAS EMPTY ON ONE SIDE, SO I PUT THE PUP IN THERE. I TIED THE LANTERN TO ONE CORNER SO THE PUP COULDN'T TURN IT OVER AND START A FIRE. I FIGURED IT WOULD KEEP THE PUP WARM AND COZY.

Since Bell was just fresh and full of co-lostrum, and the pup needed colostrum, I would feed the pup milk from Bell. Getting the milk from Bell wasn't a problem; the problem came when I tried feeding it to the pup. First, I tried dropping it into her mouth, using my finger. I knew I could never get enough milk in her that way to fill her up. Then, I got an oat straw that was hollow and sucked the milk up in it, then let it dribble into her mouth. I saw that this would work, at least till I could come up with a better way.

Now I started worrying about Sally. I had never lied to her before. What was she going to say when she found out that I hadn't killed the wolf pup? I decided to deal with it when the time came. All I knew was that I couldn't take the pup's life after saving it only moments before! I wished I hadn't cut the wolf open at all. I found myself torn between my love for Sally and my conscience. I only hoped Sally would understand that, when the time came.

That night we didn't speak. We went to bed and I lay there thinking about Sally and our growing family. We'd been married for three years and had a son, Jake, eighteen months old, and another baby on the way. Sally figured the baby would be born in late August, and since it was only the middle of February, it would be another six months.

IT WAS 1932 AND WE LIVED IN A TWO-ROOM LOG CABIN WITH A FIREPLACE. ABOUT A HUNDRED YARDS IN FRONT OF THE HOUSE WAS THE BARN WHERE WE KEPT THE GRAIN, THE HARNESS FOR THE TEAM, AND THE WAGON, AND AT NIGHT, WE'D KEEP THE MILK COWS THERE AS WELL.

JUST TO THE SOUTH OF THE BARN WAS THE CHICKEN COOP WHERE THE BLACK WOLF HAD GRABBED THE CHICKEN. THE CORRAL STARTED AT THE CHICKEN COOP AND WENT BEHIND THE BARN, AND THEN AROUND TO THE OTHER SIDE.

THE NEXT MORNING, SALLY DIDN'T TALK MUCH. I FIGURED SHE WAS STILL UPSET. I DID THE CHORES AND MILKED BELL. THE PUP WAS SURE GLAD TO GET SOME MILK. I FED HER WITH A PIECE OF OAT STRAW AGAIN. I KNEW I HAD TO FIND A BETTER WAY OF FEEDING HER, AND I SPENT THE BETTER PART OF THE DAY TRYING TO COME UP WITH SOMETHING.

I SEARCHED TILL I FOUND A SMALL EMPTY BOTTLE. I TOOK A PIECE OF THIN LEATHER AND TIED IT AROUND THE TOP OF THE BOTTLE, THEN CUT A SMALL HOLE IN THE CENTER OF IT. I PULLED THE SOFT LEATHER AWAY FROM THE BOTTLE TO FORM THE SHAPE OF A NIPPLE. THAT NIGHT, THE PUP TOOK IT LIKE IT WAS THE REAL THING!

I FED THE PUP FRESH, WARM MILK TWICE A DAY, AND EACH TIME SHE TOOK MORE.

AFTER TWO WEEKS, HER EYES WERE FULLY OPEN. SHE WAS GROWING LIKE A WEED, AND I SPENT A GOOD BIT OF TIME PLAYING WITH HER. SHE WAS OLD ENOUGH

8

NOW THAT SHE DIDN'T NEED THE LANTERN FOR HEAT.

WHILE I WAS DOING THE CHORES, I'D TURN HER LOOSE IN THE BARN AND LET HER RUN. SHE ALWAYS WANTED ME TO PET HER, AND SHE REALLY LOVED IT WHEN I SCRATCHED HER BELLY. EVERY TIME I PUT HER BACK IN THE BOX, SHE WHINED. SHE WANTED TO STAY WITH ME; SHE DIDN'T LIKE BEING ALONE.

I STARTED TYING HER UP AND LEAVING HER IN THE OPEN PART OF THE BARN. THE FIRST TIME I TRIED IT, I THOUGHT SHE WOULD THROW A FIT, BUT SHE DIDN'T SEEM TO MIND AT ALL. SHE WAS A RIGHT SMART PUP, AND I KNEW I WAS GETTING TOO ATTACHED TO HER.

SHE WAS NOW AROUND THREE WEEKS OLD, AND EVERY TIME I WALKED INTO THE BARN, SHE'D START WHINING AND YAPPING; GETTING ALL EXCITED! I KNEW SALLY WOULD FIND HER BEFORE LONG.

IT WAS NOW EARLY MARCH. THE WEATHER WAS WARMING UP AS WINTER WAS LOSING ITS GRIP AND SALLY WOULD BE OUTSIDE MORE. I KNEW SHE'D BE ABLE TO HEAR THE PUP YAPPING AND WHINING. THE PUP WAS DRINKING MILK BY HERSELF, AND SHE COULD SURE PUT IT AWAY!

THE NEXT MORNING, I TURNED HER LOOSE, AND SHE WAS RUNNING AROUND THE BARN WHILE I WAS CHORING. THEN, THE BARN DOOR OPENED AND IN WALKED SALLY! SHE SAW THE PUP FIRST THING AND ASKED, "IS THAT THE WOLF PUP YOU WERE SUPPOSED TO HAVE DROWNED?"

I SAID, "YES, SALLY, IT IS." SHE WHIRLED

AROUND AND STORMED OUT OF THE BARN!

IN JUST A FEW MINUTES SHE WAS BACK WITH THE RIFLE. SHE HANDED IT TO ME AND DEMANDED, "GET RID OF THAT WOLF -- NOW!"

I SAID, "SALLY, I CAN'T KILL THAT LITTLE PUP! I COULDN'T KILL HER WHEN I FIRST BROUGHT HER HOME, AND I CAN'T KILL HER NOW. I LOVE YOU MORE THAN ANYTHING IN THIS WORLD, BUT MY CON-SCIENCE WON'T LET ME KILL HER."

SHE SAID, "THEN I'LL KILL IT!" SHE SNATCHED THE RIFLE OUT OF MY HAND AND CAUGHT THE PUP, THEN STORMED OUT OF THE BARN, ADDING, "YOU WATCH JAKE UNTIL I GET BACK!"

I STOOD THERE AND WAITED FOR THE SHOT. AFTER SEVERAL MINUTES, I STILL HADN'T HEARD ANY-THING. THEN THE BARN DOOR OPENED AND SALLY WALKED IN. SHE WAS HOLDING THE PUP IN HER ARM, AND IT WAS LICKING HER ON THE FACE. TEARS WERE RUNNING DOWN HER CHEEKS. THAT PUP HAD TORN A HOLE IN HER HEART! SHE LOOKED AT ME AND ASKED, "WHAT'S HER NAME?"

"SHE DOESN'T HAVE ONE," I ANSWERED.

SHE SAID, "WE CAN'T HAVE A PUP WITHOUT A NAME. I GUESS WE'LL JUST HAVE TO GIVE HER ONE." SHE PICKED UP JAKE, AND WITH HIM IN ONE ARM AND THE WOLF PUP IN THE OTHER, SHE WENT BACK TO THE HOUSE. A BIG LUMP CAME UP IN MY THROAT AS I HELD BACK THE TEARS. I'D BE ABLE TO DO MY WORK NOW WITHOUT HAVING TO WORRY ABOUT SALLY AND THE PUP.

That night after supper, Sally said, "I have a good name for the pup."

"What's that?" I asked.

"We'll call her Lucky," she said, "because she's lucky to be alive."

I smiled and said, "I like that name,2 it fits her." So we started calling her Lucky, and by the time she was six weeks old, she knew her name.

Jake and Lucky became good buddies and were inseparable. Jake would put Lucky in his bed every night, and Sally would put her down after Jake went to sleep; but every morning, Lucky was back on the bed. We didn't know if she got up there on her own or if Jake was putting her up there during the night. It never failed -- Lucky was always on Jake's bed every morning.

We really hadn't realized how close the two had become until Sally tried to feed Lucky while Jake was sitting at the table, and Lucky wouldn't eat. Sally said, "Lucky must not be feeling well."

I asked, "What do you mean?"

She said, "She won't eat."

Jake said, "I feed ucky," and got off his chair and handed Lucky her bowl. She gobbled it up! We both sat there totally amazed! We couldn't believe what had just taken place.

I said, "Try feeding her again in the morning and see if she'll eat for you."

THE NEXT MORNING, AT BREAKFAST, SALLY TRIED TO FEED LUCKY, AND AGAIN, SHE WOULDN'T EAT. I TOOK THE BOWL AND TRIED FEEDING HER, AND SHE WOULDN'T EAT FOR ME, EITHER. THEN JAKE HANDED HER THE BOWL AND SHE ATE HER FOOD.

WE STARTED WATCHING JAKE AND LUCKY A LOT CLOSER. THEY WERE ALWAYS PLAYING GAMES. THE TWO GAMES THEY SEEMED TO LIKE MOST WERE "CATCH ME IF YOU CAN" AND "TUG OF WAR." LUCKY WOULD CHASE JAKE AROUND AND AROUND THE YARD AND THEN KNOCK HIM DOWN SO HE WOULD WRESTLE WITH HER. THEN, JAKE WOULD CHASE LUCKY, AND SHE'D ACTUALLY LET HIM CATCH HER SO THEY COULD WRESTLE SOME MORE. SHE HAD TO BE THE SMARTEST ANIMAL I'D EVER SEEN!

I LOVED TO WATCH THEM PLAY "TUG OF WAR." WHEN LUCKY WANTED TO PLAY, SHE'D FIND A RAG AND TAKE IT TO JAKE. WHEN JAKE TOOK HOLD OF IT, THE BATTLE WAS ON! LUCKY WOULD GROWL, SHAKE HER HEAD AND PULL. THOSE TWO WOULD PLAY TILL THEY WERE COMPLETELY EXHAUSTED! THEY WERE NEVER MORE THAN A FEW FEET APART, AND WHEN THEY RESTED, THEY RESTED TOGETHER.

LUCKY WAS NOW SIX MONTHS OLD AND ALMOST AS BIG AS JAKE. WE WERE WONDERING HOW SHE'D ACT TO-WARD THE NEW BABY. IT WAS DUE TO ARRIVE AT ANY TIME. I FIGURED LUCKY WOULD ACCEPT THE BABY, JUST LIKE SHE HAD ACCEPTED JAKE.

Two

Lucky Answers the Call

We named the baby "Tom." After he was born, Lucky wouldn't get near Sally. I'd come in the house several times a day to check on Sally and our new son. One afternoon when I came in, Jake and Lucky were lying on the floor and Jake was asleep. I reached down to pick him up so I could put him on the bed and Lucky growled at me; she wasn't going to let me touch him. Then he woke up just enough that Lucky let me pick him up and put him on the bed. This concerned me very much. Now I wondered how she would act toward the baby.

As time passed and the baby grew stronger, Lucky would get close to him and smell him. We figured she was establishing an identity for Tom. Wolves, with their acute sense of smell, identify everything that way.

When Tom got old enough to start crawling, Lucky would lie and watch him. If he started crawling toward the fireplace, she would lie down in front of him to keep him from getting too close. She did the same thing if he started toward the door.

13

LUCKY, NOW A YEAR OLD, WAS ALMOST FULL GROWN. JAKE HAD LEARNED TO RIDE HER AND SHE SEEMED TO ENJOY IT. SHE WOULD WALK AROUND WITH HIM ON HER BACK AND HIS ARMS AROUND HER NECK. SHE NEVER TRIED TO RUN; SHE WOULD ONLY WALK, AND JAKE WOULD LAUGH TILL HE CRIED.

TOM WAS NOW CRAWLING GOOD. HE WOULD CRAWL UP TO LUCKY, THEN REACH UP AND GRAB HER HAIR WITH BOTH HANDS AND PULL HIMSELF UP. SHE DIDN'T SEEM TO MIND.

THE LAST WEEK OF FEBRUARY, SALLY MENTIONED HOW MUCH SHE WAS LOOKING FORWARD TO HAVING FRESH VEGETABLES TO EAT. I PUT TOM DOWN AND WENT TO THE SMOKEHOUSE THAT I'D BUILT LATE LAST FALL, BEFORE WINTER WEATHER HAD SAT IN. I SURE WAS GLAD WE HAD THE PIGS. I PLANNED ON BUTCHERING A COUPLE WHEN THE FIRST COLD SNAP HIT. I FIGURED IT'D BE SOMETIME AROUND THE LAST OF NOVEMBER. THEY'D SURE LOOK GOOD HANGING IN THE SMOKEHOUSE THIS WINTER, AFTER I GOT THEM FATTENED UP, AND THEY'D TASTE EVEN BETTER!

STANDING THERE LOOKING AT THE HIGH POLES I'D FIXED TO HANG MEAT ON, I COULD SMELL THOSE DRIED BEANS AND HAM HOCK COOKING!

I REMEMBERED SALLY'S COMMENT ABOUT FRESH VEGETABLES, SO I WENT TO THE SIDE SHED OF THE BARN TO CHECK MY GARDEN SEED AND SEE WHAT I'D NEED TO BUY FOR PLANTING THE GARDEN.

THE NEXT MORNING, I DID ALL THE CHORES EARLY, THEN HITCHED THE HORSES TO THE WAGON. THE

SUN WAS SHINING AND I FIGURED I'D GO INTO TOWN AND GET SOME SUPPLIES WE WERE NEEDING. I WOULD ALSO PICK UP SOME SEED FOR THE GARDEN AND THE FIELD CROPS I'D BE PLANTING.

SALLY WAS GETTING CABIN FEVER. SHE SAID, "WOULD YOU TAKE JAKE WITH YOU SO I CAN HAVE A LITTLE BREAK?"

I SAID, "GET YOUR COAT AND HAT, JAKE. WE CAN HAVE A REAL GOOD TIME! LET'S ASK LUCKY IF SHE WANTS TO GO ALONG."

JAKE GOT HIS HAT AND COAT OFF THE PEG BY THE DOOR AND PUT THEM ON, STRUGGLING TO GET HIS COAT BUTTONED STRAIGHT. HE TURNED TO LUCKY AND SAID, "LUCKY, YOU WANT TO GO TO TOWN WITH US?" LUCKY SHOWED HER TEETH, IN AN APPARENT GRIN, THEN WALKED OVER TO THE DOOR AND WAITED FOR JAKE TO OPEN IT.

AS WE HEADED OUT THE DOOR, SALLY SAID, "MAKE SURE JAKE KEEPS HIS HAT ON. I DON'T WANT HIM TO GET AN EARACHE."

I SAID, "HE'LL BE FINE!" WE CLIMBED IN THE WAGON AND HEADED FOR TOWN.

WHEN WE STOPPED IN FRONT OF THE GENERAL STORE, I SAID, "JAKE, YOU'D BETTER MAKE LUCKY STAY IN THE WAGON. I DOUBT IF MR. PARKER WOULD LIKE IT IF WE WENT INTO HIS STORE WITH A BIG, BLACK WOLF ALONGSIDE US; WE'D SURE SEND HIS CUSTOMERS FLYING! I IMAGINE HE'D GET A MITE UPSET!"

I GOT DOWN AND HELD OUT MY ARMS. JAKE POINTED HIS FINGER AT LUCKY AND TOUCHED HER ON

THE NOSE. HE SAID, "STAY, LUCKY, STAY!" SHE
LOWERED HER TAIL AND SAT DOWN. JAKE PATTED HER
ON THE HEAD AND SAID, "GOOD GIRL, LUCKY," THEN
TURNED AND JUMPED INTO MY UPRAISED ARMS. I
CAUGHT HIM AND STOOD HIM BESIDE ME. HE TOOK ONE
LONG LOOK AT LUCKY AND WENT WITH ME INTO THE
STORE.

WE SPENT ABOUT THIRTY MINUTES GATHERING UP
OUR SUPPLIES AND SEED. MR. PARKER ALWAYS LET ME
CHARGE MY SUPPLIES TILL FALL WHEN I GOT MY CROPS
IN. HE WAS HANDING JAKE A PIECE OF HOREHOUND
CANDY WHEN I HEARD A BIG COMMOTION OUTSIDE. I
RAN OUT AND SAW TWENTY-FIVE OR THIRTY -- PEOPLE;
YOUNG AND OLD ALIKE -- GATHERED AROUND MY WAGON.
A COUPLE OF BOYS WERE POKING STICKS AT LUCKY, AND
THE BLACK HAIR ON HER BACK WAS STANDING STRAIGHT
UP! HER LIPS WERE SNARLED AND A LOW, WARNING
GROWL WAS COMING FROM HER THROAT!

I STEPPED IN FRONT OF THE TWO BOYS AND
SAID, "YOU BOYS PUT THOSE STICKS DOWN AND QUIT
TEASING LUCKY. SHE'S GUARDING MY WAGON; SHE'S
JUST DOING HER JOB."

THE BOYS DROPPED THEIR STICKS AND WALKED
OFF, DISAPPOINTED BECAUSE THEIR FUN HAD BEEN IN-
TERFERED WITH. AS THE REST OF THE CROWD MOVED
AWAY, I HEARD COMMENTS LIKE "WHAT KIND OF FAMILY
WOULD HAVE A BLACK WOLF FOR A PET?"

I STROKED LUCKY ON THE HEAD TO CALM HER
DOWN. WHEN I WAS SATISFIED THAT EVERYTHING WAS
UNDER CONTROL, I WENT BACK INSIDE THE STORE TO

GET JAKE AND OUR SUPPLIES. WE LOADED THINGS ON
THE WAGON AND HEADED HOME.

WHEN WE GOT OUT OF TOWN AWAYS, LUCKY
SEEMED RELIEVED. SHE STAYED UNDER THE WAGON SEAT
MOST OF THE WAY HOME; BUT ONCE WE GOT WITHIN A
MILE OR SO OF THE CABIN, SHE CRAWLED OUT FROM
UNDER THE SEAT AND CLIMBED UP BESIDE JAKE. SHE
WAS IN FAMILIAR TERRITORY NOW.

WE PLANTED THE GARDEN AND CELEBRATED
SALLY'S BIRTHDAY THE NEXT WEEK. I PLANTED THE
FIELD CROPS, AND FROM TIME TO TIME, I HOED THE
GARDEN. AS SUMMER CAME AND WENT, SALLY KEPT THE
VEGETABLES PICKED AND CANNED EVERYTHING SHE COULD
FOR THE WINTER AHEAD.

IN LATE MAY, TOM WAS NINE MONTHS OLD AND
WAS ABLE TO SCOOT OFF THE BED BACKWARD WITHOUT
FALLING. WE DECIDED HE WAS OLD ENOUGH TO START
SLEEPING WITH JAKE. AT FIRST, WE WERE A LITTLE
CONCERNED ABOUT LUCKY AND HOW SHE MIGHT REACT.
WE WATCHED HER CLOSELY. SHE DIDN'T SEEM TO MIND
AT ALL. THE ONLY DIFFERENCE WE COULD SEE BETWEEN
JAKE AND THE REST OF US WAS HER EATING. SHE
WOULDN'T TAKE FOOD FROM ANYONE BUT JAKE. WE'D
GIVE TOM SMALL PIECES OF MEAT TO FEED HER, BUT
SHE WOULDN'T TAKE IT. THEN JAKE WOULD TRY IT AND
SHE'D EAT IT. WE KNEW LUCKY WOULD TOLERATE
EVERYONE IN THE FAMILY, BUT JAKE WAS HER MASTER.

IT WAS EARLY SEPTEMBER, AND LUCKY SPENT
ALMOST ALL OF HER TIME OUTSIDE. SHE'D GIVE OUT
LONG, LONESOME HOWLS, AND I KNEW SHE WAS BEING

17

INFLUENCED BY HER NATURAL INSTINCTS; I FELT SHE WAS LONGING TO BE WITH HER OWN KIND.

As time passed, Lucky grew more and more restless. Sally began noticing it, too. Lucky seemed more restless at night when the wolves were howling than at any other time. As long as the boys were playing with her, she seemed content.

I said, "Sally, I'm afraid we're going to lose Lucky to the wild one day." She agreed, knowing I was right.

Winter was over now, and Lucky was more restless than ever. She was torn between the love of the only family she'd ever known and the call of the wild. One night she was pacing the floor, frantically. Then she started scratching at the door. I let her out and she never returned.

The boys couldn't understand why Lucky didn't come home. They cried themselves to sleep every night for a month or more. I kept hoping and believing that Lucky would come back, but the more time that passed, the more I felt we'd never see her again. Every time I'd hear a wolf howl, I wondered if it was Lucky.

After a time, I gave up on her ever coming home again. I told the boys I would get them a dog, but they said, "If we can't have Lucky, we don't want anything!"

I realized now, more than ever before, just how much Lucky really meant to them.

It was now late winter, 1935. Tom was two and a half and Jake was four and a half. It seemed that Tom had forgotten all about Lucky, and Jake didn't talk about her much. She had been gone for almost a year.

I said, "Sally, I think I'll try to find a dog for the boys."

She said, "I don't think we'll ever be able to replace Lucky."

Well, I knew we couldn't replace her, but I also knew the boys needed a dog.

Another month passed and I still hadn't found a dog for the boys. It was late March and the weather was warming up. We had already started planting the garden, and it would soon be time to plant the field crops.

One afternoon a few days later, I was in the barn repairing some harness and Sally was in the house. The boys were playing outside. Suddenly, they started screaming at the tops of their lungs! I whirled around and ran out the barn door at the same time Sally raced out of the house. It was Lucky! She had come home!

She was licking the boys on the face, and they were hugging her, and both of them were crying. Tears came to my eyes as I reached the boys and Lucky, I could see that Sally was crying, too.

We stood in the yard, petting her for awhile, and then Sally went into the house and

19

GOT HER A BIG BOWL OF MILK. LUCKY LAPPED IT UP!
SHE ACTED LIKE SHE WAS STARVED! I KNEW SHE WAS
NURSING PUPS; SHE WAS AS THIN AS A RAIL! SALLY
GAVE HER MORE MILK AND A LITTLE LEFTOVER ROAST.

LUCKY WOULDN'T GO IN THE HOUSE. I THINK
SHE WAS AFRAID WE'D SHUT THE DOOR AND NOT LET HER
OUT. AFTER AN HOUR OR SO, SHE RAN BACK TOWARD
THE WOODS. JAKE CALLED TO HER, BUT SHE KEPT
GOING. WHEN SHE REACHED THE EDGE OF THE CLEAR-
ING, SHE STOPPED AND LOOKED BACK, THEN DISAPPEARED
INTO THE WOODS.

THE NEXT AFTERNOON, SHE CAME TO THE HOUSE
AGAIN. WE FED HER AND SHE STAYED AND PLAYED WITH
THE BOYS FOR A COUPLE OF HOURS BEFORE GOING BACK
TO THE WOODS.

EVERY DAY AT ABOUT THE SAME TIME, LUCKY
WOULD SHOW UP. SHE WOULD STAY FOR A COUPLE OF
HOURS AND EAT WHATEVER SALLY GAVE HER, THEN LEAVE.

THIS WENT ON FOR ABOUT A WEEK. THEN ONE
DAY SHE BROUGHT WITH HER, FIVE WOLF PUPS. FOUR
WERE GRAY AND ONE WAS SOLID BLACK! THE PUPS WERE
AFRAID OF US AT FIRST; BUT AFTER A FEW MINUTES,
THEY LET US PET THEM.

NO ONE WANTED ANYTHING TO DO WITH ANY OF
THEM BUT THE BLACK ONE. TOM AND JAKE BEGGED,
"LET'S KEEP IT! PLEASE, DADDY, LET'S KEEP IT!"

I SAID, "IF LUCKY WANTS US TO HAVE IT,
SHE'LL LEAVE IT."

I FIGURED THE PUPS TO BE ABOUT FIVE WEEKS
OLD. WHEN SALLY PUT OUT THE MILK, THEY DRANK

20

THEIR SHARE. IT MADE SALLY FEEL GOOD WHEN LUCKY ATE WHATEVER SHE FED HER, BECAUSE SHE HAD NEVER EATEN FOR HER BEFORE.

AFTER ABOUT AN HOUR OF PLAYING, LUCKY STARTED YAPPING TO HER PUPS AND THEY GATHERED ROUND HER. I PICKED UP THE BLACK ONE AND HELD IT IN MY ARMS AS THEY STARTED OFF. LUCKY AND THE OTHER PUPS WERE ONLY A FEW FEET AWAY WHEN SHE CAME BACK AND, WITH HER MOUTH, TOOK THE BLACK PUP BY THE NAP OF THE NECK AND PULLED IT FROM MY ARMS. SHE CARRIED IT SEVERAL FEET BEFORE SETTING IT DOWN, THEN LED ALL THE PUPS INTO THE WOODS.

THE NEXT DAY, LUCKY CAME BACK. THIS TIME, SHE HAD ONLY ONE PUP WITH HER -- THE BLACK ONE! SHE DIDN'T STAY LONG. SHE DRANK THE MILK, AND WHILE THE BOYS WERE PLAYING WITH THE PUP, SHE RAN TO THE EDGE OF THE CLEARING. SHE STOOD THERE AND LOOKED BACK FOR A LONG TIME BEFORE DISAPPEARING INTO THE WOODS, NEVER TO BE SEEN AGAIN.

Three

Spike Goes to School

THE PUP REALLY TOOK TO THE BOYS AND PLAYED WITH THEM TILL DARK, THEN HE STARTED WHINING; HE WAS MISSING HIS MOTHER. THIS LASTED FOR ONLY A FEW DAYS; THE BOYS KEPT THE PUP SO BUSY PLAYING, IT DIDN'T HAVE MUCH TIME TO THINK ABOUT ITS FAMILY IN THE WILD.

I ASKED THE BOYS WHAT THEY WERE GOING TO CALL THE PUP. I TOLD THEM IT NEEDED TO BE A BOY'S NAME, BECAUSE THE PUP WAS A MALE. WE ALL THOUGHT ABOUT WHAT TO CALL HIM.

THAT NIGHT, WHILE SALLY WAS BUSY COOKING SUPPER, THE BOYS WERE PLAYING WITH THE PUP. SHE NOTICED THAT THEY WERE PLAYING WITH ONE OF HER GOOD POT HOLDERS, AND WHEN SHE REACHED DOWN TO GET IT, THE PUP GRABBED HER BY THE ARM, WANTING TO PLAY WITH HER, TOO. SHE PUSHED HIM AWAY AND SAID, "I'M TOO BUSY TO PLAY WITH YOU RIGHT NOW; I'VE GOT TO COOK SUPPER."

THE PUP'S TEETH WERE SO SHARP, THEY'D LEFT TOOTH MARKS ON HER ARM. HE WAS JUST PLAYING, BUT YOU COULD SEE THE MARKS LEFT BY HIS TEETH. SALLY SAID, "HIS LITTLE TEETH ARE LIKE SPIKES! IF HE WAS A MIND TO, HE COULD TEAR YOUR ARM OFF!"

23

I SAID, "SALLY, I THINK YOU JUST NAMED THE PUP!"

"WHAT?" SHE ASKED.

I SAID, "SPIKE!"

SALLY AND THE BOYS THOUGHT SPIKE WAS A GOOD NAME, SO WE CALLED THE PUP SPIKE FROM THEN ON.

SPIKE AND THE BOYS BECAME INSEPARABLE. IF THE BOYS HAD TO GO IN DIFFERENT DIRECTIONS, SPIKE HAD A HARD TIME DECIDING WHICH ONE TO GO WITH. IT SEEMED TO BE FIRST WITH ONE, THEN THE OTHER. WE KNEW HIS LOYALTY WAS TO BOTH BOYS.

IN LATE AUGUST, JUST BEFORE TOM'S THIRD BIRTHDAY, THE BOYS AND SPIKE WERE PLAYING AT THE NORTH END OF THE HOUSE. SPIKE, LIKE LUCKY, LIKED TO PLAY "CATCH ME IF YOU CAN" AND "TUG OF WAR." WE KEPT THE KINDLING FOR THE COOK STOVE PILED UP CLOSE TO THE HOUSE, ON THE NORTH SIDE. SALLY HOLLERED TO JAKE TO BRING HER AN ARMLOAD OF KINDLING.

I WAS NEARBY, REPAIRING THE RIM ON THE HUB OF THE WAGON WHEEL, AND I HEARD SPIKE GROWL. I LOOKED UP JUST IN TIME TO SEE HIM JUMP -- WHAT LOOKED TO BE RIGHT ON TOP OF JAKE! JAKE SCREAMED AND SPIKE STARTED SLINGING HIS HEAD FROM SIDE TO SIDE! I FROZE FOR A SPLIT SECOND AND THEN SAW THAT SPIKE HAD A SNAKE IN HIS MOUTH! I RAN TO THE BOYS AND PULLED THEM BACK A SAFE DISTANCE, THEN GOT A CLUB TO HELP SPIKE KILL THE SNAKE. HE WOULD SHAKE THE SNAKE FOR AWHILE, THEN TURN IT

LOOSE, THEN GRAB IT AND SHAKE IT AGAIN. THE NEXT
TIME HE DROPPED IT, I TOOK THE CLUB TO IT AND
BEAT IT TO DEATH! SPIKE HAD ALMOST KILLED IT AL-
READY. ALL I DID WAS FINISH IT OFF!

I RAN TO JAKE AND ASKED, "DID IT BITE YOU,
SON?"

HE SAID, "NO, DADDY." I CHECKED HIM OVER
TO BE SURE, THEN TURNED AND LOOKED AT SPIKE,
THINKING HOW GRATEFUL I WAS FEELING RIGHT NOW.
HE HAD PROBABLY SAVED JAKE'S LIFE.

SPIKE WAS PAWING AT HIS MOUTH. WHEN I
CHECKED HIM, I SAW THAT THE SNAKE HAD BITTEN HIM
ON THE UPPER LIP. SINCE IT WAS A COPPERHEAD, I
KNEW HE'D GET REAL SICK! COPPERHEAD BITES WOULD-
N'T USUALLY KILL A DOG OR A WOLF, BUT IT WOULD
MAKE THEM VERY SICK.

WE KEPT WATCHING SPIKE. BY NIGHTFALL, HIS
HEAD WAS SWOLLEN ALL OVER AND HE WAS SICK AND UN-
ABLE TO EAT. WE TRIED SEVERAL TIMES TO GET HIM
TO COME INTO THE HOUSE, BUT HE WOULDN'T.

THE NEXT MORNING, HE WAS GONE. WE
SEARCHED THE FARM OVER, BUT HE WAS NOWHERE TO BE
FOUND. I SAID, "SALLY, WITH SPIKE BEING SO
YOUNG, THERE WAS PROBABLY MORE POISON IN THAT
SNAKE THAN HE COULD HANDLE. I THINK HE HAS RUN
OFF TO DIE." BUT WHEN THE BOYS GOT UP AND ASKED
WHERE SPIKE WAS, I SAID, "SPIKE IS VERY SICK FROM
THE SNAKEBITE, AND HE'S PROBABLY GONE OFF SOME-
WHERE TO GET WELL."

ONE MORNING, AFTER SPIKE HAD BEEN GONE FOR

25

SIX DAYS, I WALKED OUTSIDE AND HE WAS LYING ON
THE PORCH. I KNEW HE MUST BE STARVED; HE LOOKED
LIKE HE HADN'T EATEN ANYTHING SINCE HE'D LEFT.
I CALLED TO SALLY AND SHE BROUGHT HIM SOME
BISCUITS AND GRAVY AND A LARGE BOWL OF MILK. IT
DIDN'T TAKE HIM LONG TO PUT IT AWAY!

WHEN THE BOYS GOT UP, THEY WERE HAPPY TO
SEE SPIKE. THEY WANTED TO HURRY THROUGH BREAKFAST
SO THEY COULD GO OUT AND PLAY. I SAID, "RE-
MEMBER, BOYS, NO ROUGHHOUSING WITH SPIKE TILL HE
GETS HIS STRENGTH BACK."

SPIKE, BEING YOUNG, RECOVERED FAST. IN
JUST A COUPLE OF WEEKS, HE WAS AS HEALTHY AS EVER
AND EVERYTHING WAS BACK TO NORMAL.

IT GOT TO THE POINT WHERE WE COULDN'T
LEAVE SPIKE AT HOME; HE JUST WOULDN'T STAY. WE
TRIED LOCKING HIM IN THE HOUSE BUT HE JUMPED
THROUGH THE WINDOW. THEN, WE LOCKED HIM IN THE
BARN, BUT HE DUG HIS WAY OUT. I EVEN TRIED
TYING HIM UP WITH A ROPE, BUT HE CHEWED THE ROPE
IN TWO.

WHEN WE WENT TO CHURCH, SPIKE WOULD WAIT
UNDER THE WAGON. WHEN WE WENT TO VISIT THE
NEIGHBORS, HE NEVER TRIED TO ENTER THEIR HOUSE.
WHEN WE WENT TO TOWN, JAKE WOULD TELL HIM TO STAY
IN THE WAGON, AND HE WOULDN'T GET OUT OF IT.

SPIKE HAD TO BE CLOSE TO THE BOYS. AS
LONG AS HE KNEW WHERE THEY WERE, HE WAS OK. HE
AND THE BOYS WERE GROWING UP TOGETHER, AND THE
BOND THEY WERE BUILDING WOULD LAST TILL DEATH.

As summer faded away, I harvested the crops and made everything ready for winter. The chill in the air kept the boys and Spike in the house more. Usually by midday, they were on Sally's nerves and she'd send them outside to play. If it was real cold outside, she'd send them to the barn. It gave them protection from the wind.

The boys never had a problem finding a game to play, no matter where they were. When they were allowed to play in the barn, they usually played in the hay. I'd found them asleep in the hay many times. They'd play till they were completely worn out, then they'd lay down on the hay to rest and fall asleep. Spike always slept between them. I guess he wanted to be close to both of them.

Spike's hair was much thicker now. He had a full winter coat. It was a good thing, too, for the full force of winter was coming down on us. We hadn't had any snow yet -- just bitter cold. It was unusual for it to be this cold in December.

Shortly before Christmas, the weather broke and it warmed up. The temperature got up to fifty during the day and dropped to the low twenties at night. The day before Christmas we got our first snow.

When the boys looked out and saw the snow, they couldn't wait to get outside. Spike would jump into the air and grab the snowflakes.

I DECIDED TO BUILD THE BOYS A SLED. THERE WAS A SMALL KNOLL JUST TO THE SOUTH OF THE HOUSE, AND IT WOULD BE A GOOD PLACE FOR THEM TO SLIDE DOWN. THEY WOULDN'T BE ABLE TO TRAVEL MORE THAN TWENTY OR THIRTY FEET, BUT IT WOULD BE FUN.

I BUILT A SLED AND PUT A ROPE ON IT SO THEY COULD PULL IT UP THE KNOLL. I HELPED THE BOYS GET STARTED. I SHOWED THEM HOW TO PULL THE SLED UP THE KNOLL AND HOW TO GET ON IT AND GET IT MOVING. SALLY AND I COULD TELL EVERY TIME THE SLED WENT DOWN THE KNOLL. THE BOYS WOULD LAUGH SO HARD, THEY COULD BE HEARD A MILE OFF.

THAT AFTERNOON, I WAS OUTSIDE THINKING ABOUT STARTING THE CHORES AND THOUGHT I'D GET A CUP OF COFFEE BEFORE GOING TO THE BARN. I WENT INTO THE HOUSE AND POURED MY COFFEE, THEN WALKED OUT TO THE PORCH TO WATCH THE BOYS PLAY WHILE I DRANK IT. I LOOKED THEIR WAY AND WAS SURPRISED TO SEE SPIKE ON THE SLED WITH THE BOYS. WHEN THE SLED STOPPED AT THE BOTTOM OF THE KNOLL, SPIKE JUMPED OFF AND GRABBED THE ROPE IN HIS MOUTH. HE STARTED WALKING BACKWARD, PULLING THE SLED WITH THE TWO BOYS ON IT. I SIMPLY COULD NOT BELIEVE HOW SMART THAT WOLF WAS.

I DECIDED TO MAKE A HARNESS FOR SPIKE SO HE COULD PULL THE SLED WITH THE BOYS ON IT. IT TOOK THE REST OF THE DAY. SINCE LEATHER AND RIVETS ARE TWO THINGS A FARM IS NEVER WITHOUT, I HAD THE MATERIALS IN THE BARN.

THE NEXT MORNING, AFTER IT HAD WARMED UP

28

A BIT, I TOOK SPIKE AND THE BOYS OUTSIDE AND PUT SPIKE'S HARNESS ON HIM, THEN HITCHED HIM TO THE SLED. I PUT TOM ON THE SLED, THEN HAD JAKE LEAD SPIKE TO SEE IF HE COULD PULL IT. SPIKE PULLED IT LIKE IT WAS NOTHING. HE TOOK TO THE HARNESS LIKE A DUCK TAKES TO WATER. I THOUGHT IT BEST JUST TO LEAVE THEM BE AND LET THEM PLAY ON THEIR OWN.

SALLY AND I WATCHED THROUGH THE WINDOW. THE BOYS WERE BOTH ON THE SLED NOW, AND SPIKE WAS RUNNING BIG CIRCLES BETWEEN THE HOUSE AND BARN. THEY PLAYED FOR A FULL HOUR BEFORE THEY STARTED WEARING DOWN. I WENT OUT AND TOOK THE HARNESS OFF SPIKE, THEN HAD THEM GO IN THE HOUSE SO THEY COULD WARM UP. IT WOULD ALSO GIVE SPIKE A CHANCE TO REST. SALLY GAVE THE BOYS SOME HOT CHOCOLATE AND GAVE SPIKE A LITTLE MILK.

IT WASN'T LONG TILL THEY WANTED TO GO BACK OUT AND PLAY. SALLY OPENED THE DOOR FOR THEM AND THEY SAILED OUTSIDE. TOM AND JAKE JUMPED ON THE SLED, AND SPIKE GRABBED THE HARNESS IN HIS MOUTH AND STARTED PULLING. I RAN OUT AND STOPPED HIM AND SHOWED JAKE HOW TO PUT THE HARNESS ON HIM. IT WAS SIMPLE TO DO AND JAKE CAUGHT ON FAST.

SPIKE AND THE BOYS HAD MORE FUN WITH THE SLED THAN ANYTHING THEY HAD EVER PLAYED WITH. THE SNOW FINALLY MELTED, AND THEY COULDN'T UNDER-STAND WHY THE SLED WOULDN'T WORK WITHOUT SNOW. THEY TRIED HITCHING SPIKE TO IT, BUT HE COULDN'T PULL IT; IT WASN'T BECAUSE HE DIDN'T TRY.

THE BOYS WERE MAD ABOUT THE SNOW BEING
GONE, BUT IT DID SNOW TWO OR THREE MORE TIMES
THAT WINTER. AND EVERY TIME IT SNOWED, IT WAS
BACK TO THE SLED. THE LAST SNOW OF WINTER WAS
IN MID-MARCH, AND IT WAS GONE THE NEXT DAY. I
HUNG THE SLED IN THE BARN AND SOAPED DOWN SPIKE'S
HARNESS SO IT WOULDN'T DRY ROT.

SPIKE WAS NOW FOURTEEN MONTHS OLD AND
WEIGHED ABOUT A HUNDRED AND FIFTEEN POUNDS. HE
WAS A BIG WOLF! IF A STRANGER EVER MET HIM IN
THE WOODS, HE'D BE SCARED TO DEATH. HE WAS SOLID
BLACK; EVEN HIS EYES LOOKED BLACK. WHENEVER
SOMEONE GOT CLOSE TO THE BOYS, SPIKE WOULD SNARL
AND GIVE A LOW, WARNING GROWL. SOME OF OUR
NEIGHBORS SAID HE MADE CHILL BUMPS GO UP AND DOWN
THEIR SPINES.

THAT SUMMER, WHEN THE WATER IN THE CREEK
GOT WARM ENOUGH, WE TOOK THE BOYS AND SPIKE
SWIMMING. THERE WAS A WATER HOLE ABOUT A FOOT
DEEP WHERE THE BOYS COULD WADE. SALLY AND I AL-
WAYS SAT ON THE BANK AND WATCHED THEM PLAY.
SPIKE WAS ALWAYS RIGHT THERE WITH THEM. THEY
REALLY LOVED PLAYING IN THE WATER.

IT WAS NOW THE FIRST OF SEPTEMBER AND JAKE
WAS TO START SCHOOL. HE WOULD BE SIX ON THE
TWENTY-FIRST OF SEPTEMBER. SALLY FIXED HIS LUNCH
AND THEN WALKED HIM TO SCHOOL.

THE SCHOOL WAS ABOUT TWO MILES FROM THE
HOUSE AND HAD ONLY ONE ROOM. THE TEACHER TAUGHT
ALL EIGHT GRADES. NO ONE IN OUR PART OF THE

COUNTRY EVER WENT PAST THE EIGHTH GRADE.

WHEN THE TEACHER CALLED THE KIDS INSIDE, SALLY STARTED HOME. WHEN SHE TRIED TO GET SPIKE TO COME WITH HER, HE WOULDN'T. HE LAY DOWN BESIDE THE FRONT DOOR AND WOULDN'T BUDGE. SALLY FINALLY CAME HOME WITHOUT HIM.

WHEN SCHOOL WAS OUT THAT AFTERNOON, SALLY WAS WAITING OUT FRONT TO WALK JAKE HOME. JAKE AND SPIKE RAN OFF AND LEFT HER. THEY WERE HOME A GOOD FIFTEEN MINUTES BEFORE SHE GOT HOME.

AFTER THE FIRST WEEK, SPIKE HAD IT ALL FIGURED OUT! HE WALKED JAKE TO SCHOOL, AND WHEN THE TEACHER WOULD CALL THE KIDS INSIDE, HE'D COME HOME AND STAY WITH TOM TILL IT WAS TIME FOR SCHOOL TO LET OUT. THEN HE'D GO BACK TO SCHOOL AND WAIT FOR JAKE AT THE DOOR AND WALK HIM HOME. FROM THEN ON, IT WAS SPIKE'S JOB TO WALK JAKE TO AND FROM SCHOOL EVERY DAY.

Four

Spike's Law

For the next two years, there was very little change. Each day was pretty much like the day before. The seasons came and went, and the bond between the boys and Spike grew much stronger.

Tom, now six, and Jake, turning eight in about three weeks, would be starting school tomorrow and both were excited.

The next morning, Sally took them to school. After the teacher called the kids in, Sally started home and tried to get Spike to go home with her, but he was sitting beside the door and wouldn't budge. He turned his head away from her and lay down. He knew both boys were in school, and there was no way he was going to leave that door.

Spike was now three and a half and had never stayed at school all day. When Sally came home that first day of school and told me that Spike stayed at school with the boys, we became concerned about what he would do when all the kids went out to play at recess and at lunchtime. I said, "I think we should go to school and make

SURE THERE'S NOT GOING TO BE A PROBLEM WITH SPIKE AND THE OTHER KIDS. I DON'T THINK HE WOULD BOTHER ANY OF THEM AS LONG AS THEY AREN'T HURTING THE BOYS."

WHAT WE WERE REALLY AFRAID OF WAS THAT KIDS SOMETIMES ROUGHHOUSE AND CARRY ON IN FUN; AND SPIKE MIGHT NOT KNOW IT WAS ALL IN FUN AND ACTUALLY HURT SOMEONE.

THE MORE WE TALKED ABOUT IT, THE MORE WORRIED WE BECAME. WE WERE NOW WALKING AT A VERY BRISK PACE. OUR CONCERN HAD CHANGED TO FEAR.

WHEN WE APPROACHED THE SCHOOLYARD, WE COULD SEE THE KIDS PLAYING "TUG OF WAR"; AND GUESS WHO WAS ON THE END OF THE ROPE? YOU GOT IT! SPIKE WAS PULLING ON THE END OF THE ROPE, JUST HAVING THE TIME OF HIS LIFE! THERE WERE SIXTEEN KIDS IN SCHOOL THAT YEAR, INCLUDING JAKE AND TOM, AND SPIKE LOVED THEM ALL!

SALLY AND I TOLD THE TEACHER OF OUR CONCERN, SO SHE LET THE KIDS STAY OUTSIDE AND PLAY A LITTLE LONGER THAN USUAL SO THEY COULD GET USED TO SPIKE AND HE COULD GET USED TO THEM.

WE WATCHED THEM PLAY "ANTE-OVER". HALF OF THE KIDS WERE ON ONE SIDE OF THE SCHOOLHOUSE AND THE OTHER HALF OF THE KIDS WERE ON THE OTHER SIDE, AND ONE SIDE HAD THE BALL. THE SIDE WITH THE BALL HOLLERED, "ANTE," AND THE OTHER SIDE HOLLERED, "OVER," AND THE BALL WAS THROWN OVER THE SCHOOLHOUSE AND THE OTHERS TRIED TO CATCH IT. THE BALL WENT BACK AND FORTH, BACK AND FORTH.

Spike caught on fast. We saw him catch the ball four times, and each time he gave it to Jake.

Then we watched the kids play "Red Rover." After several minutes, Spike had learned that game as well, and the kids were calling him over. Sally and I went home feeling very proud that Spike was a part of our family.

The teacher was a good friend of Sally's, and we continued to visit with her from time to time to check on Spike. She said, "I'm giving Spike an A. He plays with and loves all the kids, but when school is out every day, it's strictly Jake and Tom he's partial to."

Our neighbors started stopping by to ask about Spike. They wanted to see him. They said their kids had told them about him going to school every day and how much fun they had playing with him at recess. He was getting to be well known by everyone.

One afternoon in late November, the school bell started ringing; that meant trouble! We hitchedup the wagon and headed for school to find out what was wrong.

When we got there, we learned that Gracey one of Jake's and Tom's schoolmates, didn't make it home from school. She lived only a half mile from school, and they had searched everywhere and couldn't find her.

Gracey's father was holding her rag doll.

35

HE SAID HE'D FOUND IT LYING IN THE SCHOOLYARD.

IT WAS STARTING TO GET DARK, AND WE KNEW THE CHANCES OF FINDING GRACEY IN THE DARK WERE VERY SLIM. WE QUICKLY ORGANIZED A SEARCH TEAM, AND WITH KEROSENE LANTERNS, STARTED LOOKING FOR GRACEY.

WE SEARCHED TILL ABOUT MIDNIGHT AND THEN RETURNED TO THE SCHOOL TO REORGANIZE. THE WOMEN HAD HOT FOOD AND COFFEE READY. MORE MEN HAD COME IN FROM ALL AROUND. THE NEWS ABOUT THE MISSING CHILD WAS TRAVELING FAST. WE REORGANIZED AND HEADED OUT AGAIN.

WE SEARCHED FOR THE REMAINDER OF THE NIGHT. IT WAS ALMOST DAYLIGHT BY THE TIME WE RETURNED TO THE SCHOOL. THERE WAS STILL NO WORD OF THE MISS- ING GIRL, BUT WITH DAYLIGHT COMING ON AND MORE MEN ARRIVING ALL THE TIME, OUR CHANCES OF FINDING HER WERE MUCH BETTER.

BY THE TIME WE HAD SOME COFFEE AND A BITE TO EAT, THERE WERE MORE THAN A HUNDRED MEN READY TO SEARCH FOR GRACEY. THEY HAD COME FROM MILES AROUND.

WE SEARCHED UNTIL LATE AFTERNOON, THEN MET BACK AT THE SCHOOL, AND STILL, NO ONE HAD SEEN THE MISSING GIRL. THERE WAS A COLD FRONT MOVING IN AND THE TEMPERATURES WERE ALREADY BELOW FREEZING. WE KNEW IF WE DIDN'T FIND HER BEFORE DARK, SHE WOULD DIE FROM EXPOSURE BEFORE MORNING.

AS WE WERE LEAVING THE SCHOOLYARD TO CON- TINUE OUR SEARCH, SPIKE WALKED UP WITH A PIECE OF

CLOTH IN HIS MOUTH. THE GIRL'S FATHER LOOKED AT
SPIKE AND SCREAMED, "THE WOLF HAS A PIECE OF HER
DRESS IN HIS MOUTH! HE'S KILLED HER! THAT'S WHY
WE CAN'T FIND HER!" AS HE RAISED HIS GUN TO
SHOOT, I RAN TO SPIKE AND PLACED MYSELF IN FRONT
OF HIM, SHIELDING HIM WITH MY BODY.

I YELLED, "NO! SPIKE WOULDN'T DO THAT!
DON'T YOU SEE? SPIKE HAS FOUND HER!"

ALL THE MEN SIDED WITH GRACEY'S FATHER.
THEY WERE FURIOUS AND DEMANDED THAT SPIKE BE
KILLED! I CONTINUED PLEADING WITH THEM, TRYING TO
CONVINCE THEM THAT SPIKE WAS OUR ONLY CHANCE OF
FINDING THE GIRL.

EVERYONE FINALLY SETTLED DOWN AND AGREED TO
GIVE SPIKE A CHANCE TO LEAD US TO GRACEY. IF HE
COULDN'T LEAD US TO HER, THEY WOULD KILL HIM,
KNOWING THAT HIS FAILURE TO DO SO MEANT THAT HE
HAD THE PIECE OF HER DRESS IN HIS MOUTH BECAUSE
HE HAD KILLED HER.

I SAID, "SPIKE, FIND GRACEY!" HE STOOD
THERE LOOKING AT ME, NOT MOVING. I TOOK THE
PIECE OF DRESS AND SHOOK IT IN FRONT OF HIS NOSE
AND SAID, "SPIKE, FIND GRACEY!" HE TOOK OFF WITH
AROUND A HUNDRED AND FIFTY MEN FOLLOWING HIM.
EVERY ONCE IN A WHILE, HE WOULD HAVE TO STOP AND
LET US CATCH UP.

IT WAS GETTING ON NEAR DARK, AND SPIKE HAD
LED US ALMOST FIVE MILES FROM THE SCHOOL. WE
WENT DOWN INTO A HOLLER. THERE WAS A CREEK AT
THE BOTTOM AND BLUFFS ON BOTH SIDES.

37

Spike led us to a large crevasse in the bluff and stopped. I took one of the lanterns and lowered it down inside the crevasse so I could see; and there, wedged between the rocks, was Gracey. I called to her and saw her head move. I told the others, "Spike's found her; she's alive!" Everyone started cheering and praising God.

It took around thirty minutes to get Gracey out of the crevasse. We wrapped her in two of our warm coats and took turns carrying her back to the school. It was almost ten o'clock by the time we got there. All the women were still there, waiting.

Gracey's mother took her and fed her some hot food and warm milk, then asked, "Gracey, why did you go into the holler and crawl into the crevasse?"

Gracey said, "I wanted to go see Grandma, but I got lost, and when it started getting dark, I got scared. I crawled into the crevasse so nothing could get me. The next morning, I was stuck and couldn't get out. Spike came and tried to pull me out, but he couldn't. He stayed with me for a long time and then left."

The preacher was there and took over. He explained to everyone what had happened and said, "Gracey is going to be all right. We should thank God for Spike, for it was Spike who saved Gracey's life."

WORD OF SPIKE, THE BLACK WOLF, TRAVELED FAST. PEOPLE FROM ALL OVER THE COUNTRY HEARD THE STORY OF HOW HE HAD SAVED GRACEY, AND THEY CAME FROM MILES AROUND JUST TO SEE HIM. NO ONE HAD EVER SEEN A BLACK WOLF BEFORE. THREE OR FOUR TIMES A WEEK, SOMEONE STOPPED BY OUR PLACE WANTING TO GET A PUP FROM SPIKE, IF HE EVER SIRED ANY. SEVERAL WANTED TO GET THEIR FEMALE DOGS BRED TO HIM.

ALL OF THIS ATTENTION FLATTERED SALLY AND ME, BUT IT DIDN'T SEEM TO FAZE SPIKE. HE STILL LOVED TO PLAY WITH THE KIDS, BUT HE WOULDN'T LET AN ADULT TOUCH HIM. EVERY TIME A MAN REACHED OUT TO TOUCH HIM, HE WOULD SNARL AND GIVE A LOW, WARNING GROWL; IT WAS ENOUGH TO MAKE HIM PULL HIS HAND BACK.

THE PHRASE "SPIKE'S LAW" WAS STARTED BY THE KIDS AT SCHOOL AND SOON SPREAD THROUGHOUT THE COUNTRY. THE WORDS CARRIED WITH THEM THE MEANING, "KIDS ONLY; NO ADULTS ALLOWED." THE PHRASE WAS USED WHEN THE KIDS WERE GETTING READY TO START PLAYING AND ADULTS WERE AROUND. THEY'D SAY, "SPIKE'S LAW," WHICH MEANT NO ADULTS COULD PLAY. MANY TIMES AT CHURCH, SCHOOL OR EVEN IN TOWN, I'D HEAR ADULTS ASK THE KIDS WHO WERE PLAYING, "IS SPIKE'S LAW IN EFFECT TODAY?"

SALLY AND I WERE THE ONLY EXCEPTIONS TO "SPIKE'S LAW." THE PHRASE IS STILL USED TODAY BY MANY PEOPLE IN THE HILLS OF NORTHWEST ARKANSAS.

WITH THE FULL FORCE OF WINTER ON US AND

SNOW ON THE GROUND, WE TOOK THE SLED OUT OF THE BARN. SPIKE AND THE BOYS SEEMED TO ENJOY PLAYING WITH IT THIS WINTER AS MUCH AS THEY HAD THE WINTER BEFORE.

THERE WERE SEVERAL INCHES OF SNOW ON THE GROUND AND IT WAS COLD, BUT THE WIND WASN'T BLOWING, SO WE KNEW THE KIDS WOULD STILL HAVE TO GO TO SCHOOL.

THE NEXT MORNING, THE BOYS GOT THE SLED AND HITCHED SPIKE TO IT, AND HE PULLED THEM TO SCHOOL. THEY HAD TO GET OFF WHEN THEY CAME TO A HILL. SPIKE WOULD PULL THE SLED TO THE TOP, AND THE BOYS WOULD GET BACK ON.

DURING RECESS, THE KIDS HAD A GREAT TIME TAKING TURNS ON THE SLED. AFTER THAT, EVERY TIME IT SNOWED, ALL THE KIDS WOULD MEET AT THE SCHOOL TO PLAY ON THE SLED WITH SPIKE, EVEN IF THERE WAS NO SCHOOL THAT DAY.

SPIKE WAS NOW FOUR AND DIDN'T SLEEP WITH THE BOYS ANYMORE; HE HADN'T FOR QUITE SOME TIME. THE ONLY TIME HE SLEPT IN THE HOUSE WAS ON REAL COLD NIGHTS.

HERE LATELY, WHEN THE WOLVES HOWLED, HE'D ANSWER. MANY TIMES, IT SOUNDED LIKE THEY WERE CLOSE TO THE HOUSE, BUT THEY NEVER BOTHERED ANYTHING.

THERE WERE TIMES WHEN SPIKE WOULD BE GONE WHEN WE GOT UP IN THE MORNING, BUT HE'D ALWAYS SHOW UP DURING THE DAY. WE ALWAYS THOUGHT HE WAS OUT HUNTING.

One spring morning, he was gone when I
went out to do the chores and didn't come home
till late the next day. I looked up just as he
walked out of the woods with a gray wolf. As I
watched, he came on to the house, and the gray
wolf stood and watched for a few minutes, then
ran back into the woods.

For the next week and a half, Spike was
gone more than he was home. I knew he had a
girlfriend, and I figured he had started a family.
After breeding season, things were back to normal,
and he was never gone for more than a few hours
at a time.

Spike and the boys didn't play as much now
as they used to. Jake and Tom had to accept
more responsibility. They helped with the chores
and did a lot in the garden. I wanted our kids
to learn early in life what the real world was
like.

It was September and school was starting
back. Spike went with the boys to school, and
they'd come home together. Sally and I figured
that would never change.

School had been going on for a couple of
weeks when the school bell started ringing in the
middle of the day. This meant trouble! By the
time we got there, the entire community was there.
It seemed that a small boy had wandered away from
home, and they'd been unable to find him. He'd
been missing for two days, and they wanted me to

BRING SPIKE OVER THEIR WAY TO SEE IF HE COULD HELP FIND THE BOY. HIS HOME WAS ABOUT TWENTY MILES AWAY.

THE ONLY HORSES WE HAD WERE WORK HORSES, AND I KNEW THEY WOULDN'T TAKE WELL TO A SADDLE. I DIDN'T HAVE ONE ANYWAY. I TOLD THEM I WOULD BE HAPPY TO TAKE SPIKE OVER AND SEE IF HE COULD DO SOMETHING, BUT WITH MY WAGON, IT WOULD TAKE A FULL DAY OR MORE TO GET THERE. A MAN FROM A NEARBY COMMUNITY SAID HE HAD SOME GOOD HORSES THAT WOULD GET US THERE IN SHORT ORDER; SO WE WENT TO HIS PLACE. WHEN WE GOT THERE, HE SADDLED THE HORSES AND WE HEADED OUT, WITH SPIKE CLOSE BEHIND. IT HAD TAKEN A GOOD BIT OF COAXING TO GET HIM TO LEAVE THE BOYS AND GO WITH ME.

IT WAS LATE EVENING BY THE TIME WE GOT TO THE BOY'S HOME -- ONLY AN HOUR OR SO BEFORE DARK. BACK IN THE SOUTH, A THUNDERHEAD WAS BUILDING AND IT LOOKED LIKE RAIN. I KNEW IF IT RAINED, IT WOULD BE MUCH HARDER TO FIND THE BOY, BECAUSE SPIKE WOULDN'T BE ABLE TO FOLLOW THE BOY'S SCENT.

THE SEARCH WAS CENTERED FROM THE NEARBY SCHOOL. WHEN WE WALKED IN, I SAID, "I'LL NEED SOMETHING BELONGING TO THE BOY, AND IT NEEDS TO BE SOMETHING THAT HASN'T BEEN WASHED SINCE HE HAS WORN IT."

THE BOY'S MOTHER GAVE ME A HAT AND SAID, "HE WAS WEARING IT THE DAY HE WANDERED OFF."

THE LITTLE BOY WAS ONLY FOUR, AND EVERYONE

SAID THEY DIDN'T SEE HOW HE COULD TRAVEL VERY FAR. YET HE WAS NO WHERE TO BE FOUND.

I TOOK SPIKE TO THE LAST PLACE THE BOY HAD BEEN SEEN, THEN MOVED THE HAT BACK AND FORTH IN FRONT OF HIS FACE AND SAID, "GO FIND HIM, SPIKE; FIND THE BOY!" SPIKE TOOK OFF! IT WAS ALMOST DARK AND THE SKY WAS GETTING BLACK; THE STORM WAS MOVING IN FAST!

SPIKE HAD BEEN GONE FOR ONLY A SHORT TIME WHEN TOTAL DARKNESS SET IN. I WENT BACK TO THE SCHOOL WITH THE OTHERS TO SEE IF THERE WAS ANY NEW INFORMATION. A FEW OF THE SEARCH PARTIES WERE COMING IN, BUT NO ONE HAD SEEN OR HEARD ANY-THING. THE LAST OF THE SEARCHERS DIDN'T COME IN UNTIL AROUND NINE P.M. AND THERE WAS STILL NO NEWS.

I ASKED IF ANYONE HAD SEEN SPIKE, AND THEY SAID THEY HADN'T. I FIGURED HE'D BE BACK SOON. I KNEW IF HE'D FOUND THE TRAIL, IT WOULDN'T TAKE HIM LONG TO FIND THE BOY; AND IF HE DIDN'T FIND THE TRAIL, HE'D JUST COME ON BACK.

IT WAS NOW STARTING TO RAIN -- JUST A SPRINKLE AT FIRST -- BUT EVERYONE STARTED MOVING INSIDE THE SCHOOL. IT WASN'T BIG ENOUGH TO HOLD EVERYONE, SO SOME OF THEM WENT TO A BARN JUST A SHORT WAY DOWN THE ROAD.

IN A FEW MINUTES IT WAS RAINING HARD. WE KNEW THERE WAS NO WAY WE COULD SEARCH FOR THE BOY NOW. IT WAS RAINING SO HARD WE COULDN'T SEE, NOT EVEN WITH A LANTERN.

43

After a time, everyone started drifting off toward home. They said they'd be back the next morning ar first light to help search.

The rain had turned into a full-scale electrical storm. The lightning pierced the sky and the rumbling thunder literally shook the ground! I slept in the school that night and waited for Spike, but he never showed up.

Shortly after daylight, the rain was still pouring down, but some of the men began showing up to continue the search. There was still no sign of Spike, and I was starting to get concerned. I wanted to go out and help look for the boy, but I decided I'd better wait at the school for Spike.

Late that morning, the missing boy's mother came to the school and said, "Spike came to my house early this morning. He was searching the barn, and I thought he was looking for you. I put some food on the porch. He ate it, then left."

I should have known that Spike would return to the last place he'd seen me. I knew I had to go there and wait for him, in case he went back there again to look for me.

Some of the women had brought food to the school. I said, "If Spike shows up, be sure and let me know as fast as you can." I headed for the boy's home to wait for Spike, in case he went back there.

44

Time has a way of passing slow when you're waiting, and today was proving to be one of the longest day I'd ever seen in my life.

Communication lines were set up between the house and the school for any news. There was no news at all. The search parties would come in to eat and then go out again. They said, "With the rain, we can't see very far, and we can't hear because of the rain and wind." Everyone was beginning to feel that it was hopeless.

The boy's mother was becoming a little hysterical, and his father was suffering from fatigue. He hadn't slept since the boy disappeared.

I knew this kind of situation was never easy. It was the uncertainty, the not knowing, that was hard. One can't give up hope till there's no hope left. That was what was happening now; hope was fading fast. Everyone was very emotional now, as they expressed their sorrow and sympathy to the grieving family.

The last of the search parties came in and said it was useless to search anymore till the rain stopped. They waited till the last group was in to see if there was any news. There wasn't, so they headed home.

By the time everyone was gone, it was dark. I told the family I'd like to stay till morning to see if Spike came back, but I figured since he couldn't find me when he came back the first time, he had headed for home.

I WAS AT A POINT WHERE I DIDN'T KNOW WHAT TO SAY. I DIDN'T WANT TO TRY AND CONVINCE THEM THAT IT WAS STILL A POSSIBILITY THEIR SON WOULD BE FOUND IN GOOD HEALTH; AND I WASN'T GOING TO TELL THEM IT WAS HOPELESS.

THE PREACHER AND HIS WIFE STOPPED BY ON THEIR WAY HOME FROM THE SCHOOL. HE SAID EVERYONE HAD GONE ON HOME. I WAS GLAD TO SEE HIM; I KNEW HE COULD DEAL WITH THE SITUATION HERE BETTER THAN I COULD.

THE PREACHER'S WIFE MADE A POT OF COFFEE, SOME BISCUITS AND GRAVY AND FRIED SOME HAM. WE ATE SUPPER, THEN SAT AROUND AND TALKED FOR AWHILE. PREACHERS HAVE A WAY OF COMFORTING PEOPLE IN THESE KIND OF SITUATIONS. HE WAS TELLING THE BOY'S MOTHER AND FATHER ABOUT ANOTHER SITUATION SIMILAR TO THIS ONE WHEN HIS WIFE INTERRUPTED, SAYING, "I THINK THERE'S SOMEONE AT THE DOOR."

THE PREACHER STOPPED TALKING AND WENT TO THE DOOR. HE OPENED IT, AND GOLLY BE, THERE STOOD SPIKE AND THE BOY! THE LITTLE BOY WAS HOLDING ON TO SPIKE'S HAIR WITH BOTH HANDS. HIS MOTHER SCREAMED, THEN RAN OVER AND GRABBED HIM! SHE HUGGED AND KISSED HIM, AND EVERYONE CRIED WITH JOY AND RELIEF.

THE LITTLE BOY'S MOTHER KNELT DOWN AND PUT ONE ARM AROUND SPIKE AND KISSED HIM ON THE FACE. SPIKE HAD NEVER LET ANYONE DO SOMETHING LIKE THAT BEFORE! HE MUST HAVE SENSED THE WAY SHE FELT AND DECIDED IT WAS OK.

THEY DRIED THE LITTLE BOY OFF AND CHANGED HIS CLOTHES, THEN GAVE HIM SOMETHING HOT TO EAT. THEY ASKED HIM WHERE HE'D BEEN, BUT ALL HE COULD TALK ABOUT WERE THE DOG AND THE CAVE. HE THOUGHT SPIKE WAS A DOG. THE ONLY THING WE COULD FIGURE OUT WAS THAT HE'D WALKED INTO A CAVE SOMEWHERE AND COULDN'T FIND HIS WAY OUT.

THE NEXT MORNING, SPIKE AND I HEADED HOME. ABOUT THREE WEEKS LATER, WE HEARD THAT THE LITTLE COMMUNITY WHERE SPIKE HAD FOUND THE LITTLE LOST BOY HAD BEEN RENAMED. IT WAS NOW CALLED SPIKE'S CORNER.

THAT LITTLE COMMUNITY WAS NEVER MORE THAN A STOP IN THE ROAD, BUT IT'S STILL CALLED "SPIKE'S CORNER," TODAY.

Five

The Fire

It was Saturday morning, and we were doing the chores. We had two pigs, and I asked Jake to feed them. He threw a couple of ears of corn over the fence and then opened the gate so he could put the rest of the feed in the trough. I watched, just to make sure he could handle the job without any trouble. He was doing fine, so I went on with what I had to do. About an hour later, I heard Sally holler, "Soooie pig! Soooie!"

I ran out of the barn, and the pigs were rooting up the yard! I got around them, and Sally and I tried driving them back into their pen, but they wanted nothing to do with it. I hollered for Jake and Tom, thinking they were playing out behind the house. They must have been a good ways off, for it took them a while to get there.

When the boys showed up, Spike was with them. I said, "Jake, you and Tom help us drive the pigs back into the pen." They were on one side and Sally and I were on the other. Every time we'd get the pigs close to the pen, they'd

49

TURN AND RUN RIGHT BETWEEN US AND HEAD FOR THE
WOODS. WE KNEW IF THEY EVER GOT INTO THE WOODS,
WE MIGHT NEVER SEE THEM AGAIN.

WE GOT AROUND THEM AGAIN, AND I SAID,
"TOM, GET A FEW EARS OF CORN FROM THE CORN CRIB."
HE GOT A HALF DOZEN EARS. "THROW ONE TO THEM,"
I YELLED. HE TOSSED ONE EAR IN FRONT OF THEM,
AND THEY BOTH GRABBED IT! THEN I TOLD HIM TO
THROW A COUPLE INTO THE PEN. HE THREW THEM INTO
THE PEN, AND THEY JUST STOOD THERE, LOOKING IN.

WE STARTED CLOSING IN ON THEM. WHEN WE
GOT REAL CLOSE, I HOLLERED, "SOOOIE, PIG!" THAT
SCARED THEM, BUT INSTEAD OF RUNNING INTO THE PEN,
THEY TURNED AND RAN OVER SALLY! WHEN SHE FELL TO
THE GROUND, SPIKE TOOK OFF AFTER THE PIGS! HE
GOT IN FRONT OF THEM AND GRABBED ONE BY THE NOSE!
IT FLIPPED HEAD OVER HEALS! HE TOOK OFF AFTER
THE OTHER ONE AND GRABBED IT BY THE NOSE, AND IT
WENT ROLLING ACROSS THE GROUND. ALL AT ONCE,
THEY RAN INTO THEIR PEN. THEY'D HAD ALL OF SPIKE
THEY WANTED! I SHUT THE GATE AND FASTENED IT,
THEN SAID, "JAKE, FROM NOW ON, MAKE SURE YOU FAS-
TEN THE GATE AFTER YOU FEED THE PIGS."

JAKE SAID, "YES, SIR," REALIZING THE IMPOR-
TANCE OF WHAT I'D SAID.

WE WERE SURE GLAD THOSE PIGS WERE BACK IN
THEIR PEN. THEY WERE FAT AND READY TO BUTCHER,
AND I WAS FIGURING ON DOING JUST THAT IN ABOUT
SIX WEEKS.

ON A FRIDAY MORNING, ABOUT TWO WEEKS LATER,

THE BOYS AND SPIKE WERE LEAVING FOR SCHOOL. WHEN SALLY AND I WALKED OUT ON THE PORCH TO WAVE GOOD-BYE, I SAW A CLOUD BANK BUILDING UP IN THE WEST. IT LOOKED LIKE WE COULD BE IN FOR SOME RAIN. I WENT ON TO THE BARN AND DID MY CHORES.

WHEN I HAD FINISHED WITH EVERYTHING, I WAS TAKING THE MILK TO THE HOUSE, AND I SAW FLASHES OF LIGHTNING IN THE WEST. THE CLOUDS WERE STILL BUILDING AND GETTING DARKER.

WHEN I GOT TO THE HOUSE, SALLY NEEDED SOME KINDLING. I SAID, "I'VE GOT PLENTY OF GOOD DRY STUFF. I'LL SPLIT IT INTO KINDLING FOR YOU." I WENT TO THE BARN TO GET THE AX AND GLANCED AT THE SKY AGAIN. THE CLOUDS WERE BLACK AND LIGHT-NING WAS DANCING ACROSS THE SKY OFF TO THE WEST; THE STORM WAS COMING OUR WAY. I DIDN'T LIKE THE LOOKS OF IT; I KNEW WE WERE IN FOR A BAD STORM. I WENT TO THE HOUSE AND TOLD SALLY THE KINDLING WOULD HAVE TO WAIT UNTIL AFTER THE STORM.

THE TEACHER, MRS. MILLER, WAS WATCHING THE STORM BUILD. SHE KNEW WHAT TO DO IF IT GOT BAD. IT WASN'T RAINING YET, BUT SHE KNEW THE WIND HAD PICKED UP AND WAS BLOWING HARDER, AND THE LIGHT-NING AND LOUD RUMBLE OF THUNDER SEEMED VERY NEAR. THERE WAS A FLASH OF LIGHTNING AND A LOUD CLAP OF THUNDER THAT LITERALLY SHOOK THE SCHOOL! SHE KNEW THE LIGHTNING HAD STRUCK NOT FAR AWAY, SO SHE LOOKED AT THE CHILDREN AND, WITH A FORCED CALM IN HER VOICE, SAID, "I WANT EACH OF YOU TO CLOSE YOUR BOOK AND GET UNDER YOUR DESK; DO IT NOW!"

SUDDENLY, THE WINDOW SHATTERED! THE CHILDREN SCREAMED, AND THE TEACHER LOOKED UP JUST IN TIME TO SEE SPIKE RUN TO THE DOOR AND START PAWING, WANTING OUT. SHE REALIZED THEN THAT THE WINDOW HAD SHATTERED WHEN SPIKE HAD JUMPED THROUGH IT. SHE KNEW FROM THE WAY HE WAS ACTING THAT SOMETHING WAS TERRIBLY WRONG! SHE RAN TO THE DOOR AND OPENED IT, AND SPIKE GRABBED HER DRESS AND STARTED TUGGING AT HER, PULLING HER OUTSIDE. WHEN SHE GOT OUTSIDE, SHE IMMEDIATELY SMELLED SMOKE! SHE RAN AROUND THE CORNER OF THE SCHOOL AND SAW THAT THE WOODS WERE ON FIRE!

THE LIGHTNING HAD STARTED THE FIRE AND THE WIND WAS SPREADING IT! SHE RAN BACK INSIDE AND TOLD THE KIDS TO GET OUTSIDE FAST! THEY SCRAMBLED FROM UNDER THEIR DESKS AND RAN OUT!

THE WIND WAS SPREADING THE FIRE AND THE SMOKE WAS GETTING THICK. MRS. MILLER COUNTED THE KIDS AND ONE WAS MISSING! IT WAS JOHNNY; SHE CALLED OUT, "JOHNNY!" THERE WAS NO ANSWER AND TIME WAS RUNNING OUT! THE FIRE WAS GETTING CLOSER AND THE SMOKE WAS GETTING THICK! THE KIDS WERE COUGHING AND THEIR EYES WERE WATERING. AGAIN THE TEACHER YELLED, "JOHNNY!" THERE WAS STILL NO ANSWER.

SHE WAS SCANNING THE KIDS WITH HER EYES, AND SHE SAW SPIKE WATCHING HER. SHE SAID, "SPIKE, GO FIND JOHNNY!" HE WHIRLED AND RAN BACK INTO THE SCHOOLHOUSE. JOHNNY WAS CAUGHT ON HIS DESK AND COULDN'T GET LOOSE. SPIKE GRABBED HIM,

PULLING HIM FREE, AND THEY RAN OUTSIDE.

MRS. MILLER AND THE OTHER KIDS WERE RELIEVED TO SEE THAT JOHNNY WAS ALL RIGHT. SPIKE RAN AWAYS, THEN STOPPED AND LOOKED BACK. MRS. MILLER WAS BUSY MAKING SURE THE KIDS STAYED TO-GETHER AND WASN'T LOOKING AT SPIKE, SO HE RAN BACK TO HER, TOOK HOLD OF HER DRESS WITH HIS TEETH AND PULLED. SHE LOOKED DOWN, UNDERSTANDING NOW THAT HE WANTED HER TO GO WITH HIM. SHE SAID, "LET'S FOLLOW SPIKE." HE TOOK OFF, LEADING THEM AWAY FROM THE FIRE. HE WAS MOVING FAST, IN AN APPARENT ATTEMPT TO GET THE TEACHER AND THE KIDS TO RUN, BUT THEY WERE GAGGING AND COUGHING, NOW OVERCOME BY THE SMOKE, AND THE YOUNGER KIDS WERE CRYING FOR THEIR MAMAS. SPIKE LED THEM TO-WARD THE CREEK AND AWAY FROM THE FIRE.

WHEN THEY GOT TO THE CREEK, THE TEACHER LOOKED BACK. ALL SHE COULD SEE WAS THICK, DARK GRAY SMOKE AND FIGURED THAT, BY NOW, THE SCHOOL WAS ENGULFED IN FLAMES. SHE SAW THAT THE FIRE WAS BEHIND THEM, ON THE LEFT OF THEM, AND ON THE RIGHT; THEY WERE ALMOST COMPLETELY SURROUNDED! SHE KNEW THERE WAS NOTHING SHE COULD DO EXCEPT PUT HER TRUST AND FAITH IN SPIKE. HE HAD LED THEM OUT OF THE SMOKE, BUT AS FAST AS THE FIRE WAS SPREADING, IT WOULD SOON CATCH UP WITH THEM, AND SHE DIDN'T KNOW WHICH WAY TO GO.

SPIKE LED THE TEACHER AND KIDS DOWN THE CREEK. EACH TIME THE LIGHTNING FLASHED IT STRUCK THE GROUND. AT TIMES IT WAS SO CLOSE THEY COULD

HEAR THE CRACKING OF TIMBER AS THE LIGHTNING
SLASHED AND RIPPED THE TREES APART, TURNING THEM
INTO KINDLING.

JOHNNY, THE BOY WHO HAD BEEN CAUGHT ON HIS
DESK, STUMBLED AND FELL DOWN THE FIFTEEN-FOOT BANK
AND INTO THE EDGE OF THE CREEK. HE WAS LUCKY;
HE WASN'T HURT, BUT THE BANK WAS TOO STEEP TO
CLIMB UP. HE TRIED SEVERAL TIMES TO CLIMB BACK
UP, BUT EACH TIME HE SLID BACK DOWN INTO THE
CREEK. SPIKE HAD BEEN WATCHING AND SAW THAT
JOHNNY COULDN'T GET UP THE BANK, SO HE SLID DOWN
THE STEEP BANK AND GRABBED JOHNNY'S SHIRTTAIL AND
STARTED LEADING HIM DOWNSTREAM. THE TEACHER SAW
WHAT SPIKE WAS DOING, SO SHE AND THE OTHER KIDS
WALKED ALONG THE TOP OF THE BANK STAYING EVEN
WITH SPIKE AND JOHNNY. THEY HAD TRAVELED QUITE
AWAYS BEFORE SPIKE FOUND A PLACE WHERE HE COULD
LEAD JOHNNY BACK UP ON TOP OF THE RIVER BANK
WHERE THE OTHERS WERE.

MRS. MILLER NOTICED A COUPLE OF DROPS OF
WATER HITTING HER ON THE FACE. SHE STOPPED AND
LOOKED AROUND. IT WAS STARTING TO RAIN. THAT
MEANT, IF IT RAINED HARD ENOUGH, THE FIRE WOULD
SOON BE OUT AND THEY COULD GO HOME.

ONCE IT STARTED SPRINKLING, IT DIDN'T TAKE
LONG TILL IT WAS RAINING CATS AND DOGS. WHEN THE
RAIN TURNED INTO A DOWNPOUR, THE KIDS AND THE
TEACHER TOOK REFUGE IN A SMALL CAVE WHICH WAS LO-
CATED AT THE EDGE OF A LARGE BLUFF NEAR THE
CREEK. THE LIGHTNING WAS STILL FLASHING AND THE

THUNDER WAS RUMBLING AS LOUD AS EVER, SO THEY WENT INSIDE WHERE THEY'D BE SAFE FROM THE TREACH-EROUS STORM.

BY NOW, EVERYONE IN THE COUNTY HAD SEEN THE SMOKE AND FLAMES, AND THOSE IN THE IMMEDIATE AREA KNEW IT WAS IN THE VICINITY OF THE SCHOOL. SOME KNEW THE SCHOOL HAD BURNED. THERE WAS NOTHING THEY COULD DO BUT TRY TO STAY OUT OF THE PATH OF THE SMOKE AND FIRE. THE LIGHTNING WAS FLASHING MORE THAN EVER, AND WHEN IT WOULD FLASH, IT WOULD PIERCE ONE PART OF THE SKY AND THEN TAKE OFF DANCING ACROSS IT. THE THUNDER WAS CLAPPING AND RUMBLING SO HARD THAT THE GROUND WAS VIBRAT-ING! I HAD NEVER SEEN SUCH AN ELECTRICAL STORM!

NOW THAT THE KIDS WERE SAFE, THEY WERE LAUGHING AND PLAYING GAMES. THEY STOOD NEAR THE ENTRANCE OF THE CAVE SO THEY COULD WATCH THE RAIN. SPIKE LAY DOWN AT JAKE'S FEET. HIS FRONT LEGS WERE EXTENDED STRAIGHT OUT AND HIS HEAD LAY RESTING ON THEM. JUST BY LOOKING AT HIM, YOU'D GET THE FEELING THAT HE WAS THINKING ABOUT WHAT TO DO NEXT. HE HAD A LOOK IN HIS EYES THAT IN-TRIGUED EVERYONE. SOME SAID THAT WHEN THEY LOOKED INTO HIS EYES, THEY COULD TELL WHAT HE WAS THINK-ING. THEY COULD TELL IF IT WAS OK TO TOUCH HIM OR IF THEY SHOULD LEAVE HIM ALONE.

AS THE RAIN CONTINUED, BOREDOM BEGAN SET-TING IN AND THE KIDS BECAME ROWDY AND UNRULY. THEY STARTED PUSHING EACH OTHER OUT OF THE CAVE INTO THE POURING RAIN AND OTHERS WERE THROWING

ROCKS INTO THE CREEK. THE TEACHER TRIED CALMING THEM DOWN, BUT NOTHING WORKED.

SUDDENLY, THERE WAS A BRIGHT FLASH OF LIGHTNING AND A LOUD BOOM OF THUNDER! LARGE BOULDERS BEGAN FALLING DOWN IN FRONT OF THE CAVE, AND ROCKS FELL FROM THE CEILING OF THE CAVE! THE KIDS STARTED SCREAMING AND YELLING! PAUL WAS SITTING NEAR THE ENTRANCE, AND HE SCREAMED AS A LARGE ROCK FELL FROM THE CEILING OF THE CAVE AND LANDED ON HIS LEGS!

ROCKS AND BOULDERS KEPT FALLING, DARKENING THE CAVE AS THEY BEGAN PILING UP IN FRONT OF THE ENTRANCE. THE TEACHER AND SOME OF THE OLDER KIDS RUSHED TO PAUL, AND BY THE TIME THEY GOT THE ROCK OFF HIS LEGS, THE CAVE WAS IN TOTAL DARKNESS. NOW, EVERYONE WAS SCREAMING AND CRYING, COMPLETELY HYSTERICAL.

SPIKE NEVER BARKED LIKE A DOG. THE ONLY SOUND HE EVER MADE, EXCEPT FOR A WARNING GROWL, WAS A YAPPING SOUND, LIKE A PUP. HE STARTED YAPPING AND THE CHILDREN QUIETED DOWN, LISTENING TO HIM. IT WAS AS IF THEY THOUGHT HE WAS GOING TO TELL THEM SOMETHING. AFTER THEY SETTLED DOWN, THEY STARTED USING LOGIC, WORKING TOGETHER TO MOVE SOME OF THE ROCKS THAT WERE BLOCKING THE ENTRANCE OF THE CAVE. BUT NOW THEY WERE IN TOTAL DARKNESS, AND THE PROGRESS WAS VERY SLOW.

JIMMY WAS THE OLDEST BOY. HE WAS THIRTEEN AND IN THE EIGHTH GRADE. HE TOOK CHARGE AND MOVED THE TEACHER AND ALL THE LITTLE KIDS BACK

AWAY FROM THE FALLEN ROCKS, THEN HE AND THE OTHER OLDER BOYS TRIED TO DIG THEIR WAY TO THE OUTSIDE, WORKING WAY UP INTO THE NIGHT. NOW EXHAUSTED, THEY LAY DOWN AND FELL ASLEEP.

WHEN MRS. MILLER AND THE KIDS WOKE UP, THEY WERE COLD AND HUNGRY, BUT THERE WAS NOTHING TO EAT. THE ONLY THING THEY COULD DO WAS KEEP TRYING TO DIG THEIR WAY OUT. THEY HAD NO IDEA WHAT TIME IT WAS OR WHAT THE WEATHER WAS LIKE OUTSIDE. THE OLDER BOYS CONTINUED TO MOVE DIRT AND ROCKS IN AN ATTEMPT TO FIND AN ESCAPE FROM THE TOMB IN WHICH THEY WERE TRAPPED. AFTER SEVERAL HOURS, JIMMY MOVED A LARGE ROCK AND THERE WAS A SMALL RAY OF LIGHT. HE HOLLERED, "I SEE LIGHT; I CAN SEE OUT!"

ALL THE KIDS STARTED WHOOPING AND HOLLER-ING, FOR NOW THERE WAS HOPE. JIMMY COULD NOW SEE WHAT HE WAS DOING, AND HE CONTINUED MOVING ROCKS, BEING VERY CAREFUL. HE KNEW IF HE MOVED THE WRONG ROCK, THE LARGE BOULDERS WOULD SETTLE DOWN, CLOSING THE SMALL OPENING HE'D MADE.

THE GOING WAS SLOW. THE SMALL HOLE WAS NOT YET LARGE ENOUGH FOR SOMEONE TO CRAWL THROUGH. THEN, ONE OF THE BOYS MOVED THE WRONG ROCK, AND THE LARGE BOULDERS STARTED, TO SETTLE AND ROCKS STARTED ROLLING TO THE INSIDE, PARTIALLY CLOSING THE HOLE. THE BOYS FROZE IN THEIR TRACKS, AFRAID THAT IF THEY MOVED THE WRONG ROCK, THE LARGE BOULDERS ABOVE WOULD ROLL DOWN INSIDE THE CAVE AND CRUSH THEM. SPIKE MUST HAVE SENSED THE EXTREME

DANGER EVERYONE WAS IN. HE CRAWLED UP TO THE HOLE AND SCRATCHED AND PAWED AT THE ROCKS WITH HIS FRONT FEET. THE BOYS EASED UP BESIDE HIM AND HELPED BY MOVING SOME OF THE ROCKS HE WAS PAWING AT. SPIKE KEPT PULLING THE SMALL ROCKS OUT OF THE WAY WITH HIS PAWS, MAKING THE SMALL HOLE LARGER AND LARGER. HE LAY DOWN ON HIS BELLY, AND WITH HIS HEAD AND FRONT PAWS IN THE OPENING, HE PULLED HIMSELF TOWARD THE OUTSIDE. EVERYONE HELD THEIR BREATH, AFRAID TO BREATH.

THEN SPIKE WAS THROUGH THE HOLE; HE WAS FREE! JUST AS HIS BACK LEGS CLEARED THE HOLE, ROCKS STARTED ROLLING TO THE INSIDE AND SETTLED DOWN, COMPLETELY CLOSING THE SMALL OPENING THEY'D MADE.

THEY DECIDED NOT TO DIG ANYMORE; THEY THOUGHT THE RISK WAS TOO GREAT, AND NOW WITH SPIKE ON THE OUTSIDE, HE WOULD SOON BRING HELP.

SIX

THE ATTACK OF THE BLACK BEAR

ONCE SPIKE HAD ESCAPED FROM THE CAVE, HE HEADED UPSTREAM TO LOOK FOR HELP. IT WAS STILL RAINING HARD, AND THE CREEK HAD TURNED INTO A RAGING, TREACHEROUS RIVER! HE KNEW HE NEEDED TO GET TO THE OTHER SIDE, AND EVERY FEW YARDS HE'D STOP AND LOOK AT THE RIVER, TRYING TO DECIDE IF HE SHOULD TRY AND CROSS. EACH TIME, HE DECIDED TO GO ON FURTHER UPSTREAM.

AFTER SPIKE HAD GONE ABOUT A HALF MILE, THE STREAM AND BLUFF CAME TOGETHER. THERE WAS A LARGE OUTCROPPING OF OVERHANGING ROCKS AND AS HE MADE HIS WAY UNDER THE ROCKS A BLACK BEAR AT-TACKED HIM, CATCHING HIM OFF GUARD!

THE BEAR SLAPPED SPIKE ACROSS HIS LEFT SIDE, RIPPING HIS FLESH OPEN TO THE BONE, THE SHARP CLAWS PIERCING HIS LEFT SHOULDER AND CUTTING DOWN THE FULL LENGTH OF HIS SIDE AND INTO HIS LEFT HIP. HE FELL FROM THE OUTCROPPING INTO THE WATER BELOW AND WAS CARRIED DOWNSTREAM BY THE FURY OF THE RAGING WATER! HE FOUGHT AND STRUGGLED TO GET TO THE BANK, AND AFTER SEVERAL MINUTES HE MANAGED TO DRAG HIMSELF ONTO THE BANK ON THE OTHER SIDE OF THE CREEK. HE CRAWLED A SHORT

DISTANCE FROM THE CREEK, THEN COLLAPSED. HE LAY THERE LIFELESS, BLEEDING TO DEATH.

EVERYONE IN THE COMMUNITY HAD GATHERED AT THE SCHOOL WHERE THERE WAS NOTHING LEFT BUT ASHES. THEY THOUGHT THE TEACHER AND THE CHILDREN HAD PERISHED IN THE FIRE, BECAUSE THE MAGNITUDE OF THE FIRE WAS SO GREAT AND HAD SPREAD SO FAST; THEY KNEW THAT NO ONE COULD HAVE ESCAPED ITS PATH.

SEVERAL HOMES AND BARNS HAD BEEN DESTROYED BY THE FIRE, AND AT LEAST SIX FARMERS WHO HAD BEEN UNABLE TO ESCAPE THE SMOKE AND FLAMES WERE KNOWN DEAD. IT WAS ESTIMATED THAT A THOUSAND ACRES HAD BURNED BEFORE THE RAIN PUT OUT THE FIRE.

SALLY AND I HAD LOST BOTH OF OUR SONS AND SHE WAS SEVERELY DEPRESSED, AS WAS EVERYONE WHO HAD LOST CHILDREN IN THE FIRE.

IT WAS DECIDED THAT THE FUNERAL SERVICES FOR THE FOURTEEN CHILDREN AND THE TEACHER WOULD BE HELD IN THE SCHOOLYARD AND THE PILE OF ASHES WOULD BE THEIR GRAVE. THE SERVICES WERE SET FOR TEN O'CLOCK THE NEXT MORNING.

SALLY AND I STARTED HOME, KNOWING THAT WE WERE LUCKY IN A WAY, FOR THE FIRE HAD STARTED BETWEEN OUR FARM AND THE SCHOOL, BUT BECAUSE OF THE WIND, THE FIRE HADN'T SPREAD BACK OUR WAY. AS WE PULLED INTO THE YARD AND REALIZED THAT SPIKE WASN'T HOME, IT WAS APPARENT THAT HE HAD ALSO PERISHED IN THE FIRE, FOR IF HE WERE ALIVE, HE WOULD HAVE BEEN HOME BY NOW.

In times of sorrow and grief, many people like to be alone with their memories and thoughts and Sally was such a person; and I felt it best to leave her in the house alone for awhile. I went to the barn and sat on the hay, remembering the little things the boys had done together. It seemed that every thought I had about the boys included Spike. He had become a real part of their lives from the very day Lucky brought him to us. I was so wrapped up in my thoughts that I didn't realize darkness had set in. Now, I'd have to do the chores by the light of the lantern; but, first I'd check on Sally.

As I walked into the house, she was standing over the stove cooking supper. I asked, "Sally, are you all right?"

She said, "I'm fine," then turned to me and asked, "Dave, do you think there's any chance at all that the boys are alive somewhere?"

I knew she was wanting something to hold on to, but I also knew there was no chance of anyone escaping the fire. I trembled as I said, "No, Sally; there's no chance at all. I have to do the chores now, but I'll make it fast." I left the house and went back to the barn, where I became so deep in thought while I was milking that I stopped milking and just sat there on the stool with my head resting in Bell's flank. After a spell, she twitched and brought my mind back to what I was doing. I finished milking the

61

COWS AND STARTED THE REST OF THE CHORES. WHEN I GOT THROUGH WITH EVERYTHING, I PICKED UP THE BUCKET OF MILK AND WENT TO THE HOUSE.

SALLY HAD SUPPER ON THE TABLE, SO I QUICKLY STRAINED THE MILK AND SET IT ON THE BACK PORCH; IT WAS SCREENED IN, AND THE TEMPERATURE WAS COLD ENOUGH NOW THAT IT WOULD KEEP ALL RIGHT.

AS I SAT AT THE TABLE AND ASKED THE BLESSING, IT WAS ALL I COULD DO TO KEEP BACK THE TEARS. I KNEW THAT IF I BROKE DOWN SALLY WOULD, TOO. I DIDN'T KNOW HOW THIS TRAGEDY WOULD AFFECT OUR LIVES TOGETHER. I JUST KNEW THAT I LOVED SALLY WITH ALL MY HEART AND SOUL, AND I NEVER DOUBTED HER LOVE FOR ME; BUT, WHAT WAS GOING TO HAPPEN NOW? HOW WOULD WE SURVIVE THIS TERRIBLE TRAGEDY?

SITTING THERE EATING SUPPER, IT WAS HARD TO MAKE CONVERSATION. IT SEEMED LIKE THERE WAS NOTHING TO SAY. NEITHER OF US ATE ANYTHING TO SPEAK OF; WE JUST PICKED AT OUR FOOD. AFTER SUPPER, I HELPED SALLY WITH THE DISHES. WHILE WE WERE DOING THE DISHES, SHE TURNED TO ME AND HUGGED ME, THEN BROKE DOWN AND CRIED. AFTER A TIME, SHE PULLED BACK, LOOKED ME IN THE EYE AND ASKED, "DAVE, WHAT ARE WE GOING TO DO WITHOUT THE BOYS?"

I SAID, "SALLY, WE'RE GOING TO START OVER; WE'RE GOING TO START ALL OVER."

WE FINALLY TURNED IN, BUT WE TOSSED AND TURNED ALL NIGHT; I NEVER ONCE CLOSED MY EYES, AND I DON'T THINK SALLY DID EITHER.

THE NEXT MORNING, WHILE I WAS DOING THE CHORES, SALLY'S MOM AND DAD ARRIVED AT OUR CABIN. JACK, SALLY'S DAD, CAME TO THE BARN TO TALK TO ME. HE WANTED TO KNOW HOW SALLY WAS HOLDING UP, AND I SAID, "SHE'S HOLDING UP FINE. SHE GETS HER STRENGTH AND COURAGE FROM YOU; YOU HAVE EVERY RIGHT TO BE PROUD OF HER FOR SHE HAS ALWAYS BEEN A PILLAR OF STRENGTH."

PERHAPS I SHOULDN'T HAVE TOLD JACK THAT, BUT I KNEW HIS HURT WAS DEEP, HAVING LOST BOTH GRANDSONS, AND I DIDN'T WANT HIM TO HAVE TO WORRY ABOUT SALLY. I KNEW THAT SALLY AND I WOULD MAKE IT ALL RIGHT; IT WOULD TAKE TIME, BUT WE WOULD MAKE IT.

JACK AND MARTHA LIVED ABOUT FIVE MILES AWAY, AND I KNEW THEY HAD TO HAVE LEFT WAY BEFORE DAYLIGHT TO GET HERE THIS EARLY.

WHEN I FINISHED THE CHORES, JACK AND I WENT TO THE HOUSE. SALLY AND MARTHA HAD BREAK-FAST READY. WE SAT DOWN TO EAT, KNOWING THAT THIS DAY WOULD BURN DEEP IN OUR HEARTS -- A DAY WE WOULD NEVER FORGET.

AS I LOOKED ACROSS THE TABLE AT SALLY, HER FACE LOOKED WEATHERED AND WORN. SHE LOOKED TEN YEARS OLDER, AND I FIGURED THIS KIND OF TRAGEDY WOULD AGE ANYONE. AS WE FORCED DOWN SOME FOOD, I COULDN'T HELP BUT KEEP THINKING HOW OLD SALLY LOOKED; SHE LOOKED ALMOST AS OLD AS HER MOTHER.

IT WAS NINE O'CLOCK NOW AND THE FUNERAL SERVICES WERE SET FOR TEN. WE WASHED UP A BIT

AND GOT DRESSED. JACK THOUGHT WE FOUR SHOULD RIDE TOGETHER, SO WE CLIMBED INTO HIS WAGON AND LEFT FOR THE SCHOOLYARD. IT WAS TO BE A LONG, SILENT RIDE.

I HAD ATTENDED SEVERAL FUNERALS IN MY LIFE, BUT I HAD NEVER SEEN SUCH SORROW AND MOURNING AS I SAW WHEN WE ARRIVED AT THE SCHOOLYARD. THERE WERE MOURNING PARENTS, RELATIVES AND FRIENDS OF SIXTEEN CHILDREN, ONE TEACHER AND SIX FARMERS.

THE FUNERAL SERVICES LASTED MUCH LONGER THAN USUAL, AND AFTER IT WAS OVER, EVERYONE SEEMED TO WANT TO BE ALONE. USUALLY, WHEN THERE WAS A FUNERAL, THE COMMUNITY PITCHED IN AND BROUGHT FOOD FOR THOSE IN MOURNING AND HELPED THEM WITH THEIR CHORES THAT NIGHT; BUT TODAY WAS DIFFERENT, BECAUSE EVERYONE IN THE COMMUNITY HAD BEEN AFFECTED BY THE TRAGEDY.

THIS SMALL COMMUNITY WE LIVED IN WAS CALLED OAK GROVE, SO NAMED BECAUSE OF A SMALL GROVE OF GIANT RED OAK TREES CLUSTERED TOGETHER ON A SMALL KNOLL OF RICH, FERTILE SOIL. ONCE OFF THE KNOLL, THERE WERE JUST PLAIN OAKS AND UNDERBRUSH. THE SMALL SCHOOL HAD BEEN BUILT JUST SOUTH OF THE GIANT RED OAKS. THE MIGHTY OAKS WERE PARCHED AND BLACK FROM THE FIRE, AND I WONDERED IF THEY WERE DEAD, TOO.

NOT HAVING MUCH TO SAY, EVERYONE STARTED FOR HOME. I SAW JACK AND MARTHA HEAD FOR THE WAGON, SO I LED SALLY OVER TO THE WAGON AND HELPED HER IN, THEN WE STARTED HOME.

JACK, IN AN ATTEMPT TO COMFORT SALLY, BEGAN TELLING HER ABOUT HER CHILDHOOD. HE TALKED ABOUT HOW SHE AND HER SISTERS WERE ALWAYS CLIMBING TREES, AND HOW SHE WAS ALWAYS THE LEADER. EVEN THOUGH SHE WAS YOUNGER THAN THE OTHERS, SHE WAS A NATURAL LEADER; EVEN AT SCHOOL, ALL THE KIDS LOOKED UP TO HER. SALLY AND I WERE ENGROSSED IN JACK'S STORIES, AND THE RIDE HOME DIDN'T SEEM LONG AT ALL.

WHEN WE GOT HOME, MARTHA AND SALLY WENT INTO THE HOUSE TO START DINNER, AND JACK AND I WENT TO THE BARN TO UNHARNESS THE TEAM. EVERY PLACE I LOOKED, I COULD SEE THE BOYS PLAYING, AND SPIKE WAS THERE WITH THEM. I COULD ACTUALLY HEAR THEM LAUGHING AND HOLLERING AT HIM.

NO MATTER HOW HARD I TRIED TO CONCENTRATE ON WHAT I WAS DOING, MY MIND KEPT DRIFTING AWAY. AFTER CARING FOR THE HORSES, JACK AND I HAD STARTED BACK TOWARD THE HOUSE WHEN I NOTICED SOMETHING LYING NEAR THE TREES, JUST TO THE SOUTH OF THE BARN. I POINTED IT OUT TO JACK AND ASKED, "CAN YOU MAKE OUT WHAT IT IS?"

HE SAID, "I CAN'T TELL WHAT IT IS, BUT IT'S BLACK."

WE STARTED WALKING IN THAT DIRECTION, AND AS WE GOT CLOSER, THE BLACK MASS BEGAN TO TAKE FORM. I HOLLERED, "OH GOD, IT'S SPIKE!"

I WAS RUNNING NOW, AND WHEN I REACHED SPIKE, I FELL TO MY KNEES AND LEANED OVER HIM. HE WAS LYING ON HIS RIGHT SIDE AND APPEARED TO BE

DEAD. HIS LEFT SIDE WAS RIPPED OPEN AND I COULD
SEE EVERY RIB! IT LOOKED LIKE THE WORK OF A
BEAR. I FELT OF HIS CHEST AND THOUGHT I COULD
FEEL A FAINT HEARTBEAT, BUT I WASN'T SURE. WE
CARRIED HIM TO THE HOUSE, AND AS I OPENED THE
DOOR, SALLY LOOKED AROUND AND SCREAMED. SHE RAN
OVER AND HUGGED SPIKE'S HEAD. I TOLD HER I
DIDN'T KNOW IF HE WAS ALIVE OR NOT. SHE QUICKLY
CLEARED THE KITCHEN TABLE, AND WE LAID HIM ON IT.

SALLY LOOKED AT ME AND SAID, "YOU KNOW
WHAT THIS MEANS, DON'T YOU?"

I SAID, "SALLY, IT DOESN'T MEAN WHAT YOU
THINK. IF THE BOYS WERE ALIVE, THEY WOULD HAVE
TURNED UP BY NOW."

"MAYBE NOT," SHE INSISTED.

I WAS BUSY CHECKING SPIKE AT THE TIME AND
COULD TELL THAT HE WAS BARELY ALIVE. I GOT SOME
BORIC ACID TO WASH OUT HIS DEEP WOUNDS, AND AS I
WORKED ON HIM, I COULD HARDLY BELIEVE THAT HE HAD
HELD ON THIS LONG. THE FOUR DEEP CUTS ON HIS
SIDE LOOKED TO ME LIKE THEY WERE MADE BY THE
CLAWS OF A BEAR -- A BIG BEAR. AFTER CLEANING
HIS WOUNDS, I GOT SOME CATGUT AND BEGAN STITCHING
UP THE LONG RIPS IN HIS SIDE. I REALLY DIDN'T
THINK HE WOULD LIVE AS LONG AS IT WOULD TAKE ME
TO SEW HIM UP.

I DON'T KNOW HOW, BUT SPIKE CONTINUED TO
HOLD ON. SOME SIX HOURS AND EIGHT HUNDRED AND
FORTY STITCHES LATER, JACK AND I HAD SEWN UP ALL
OF SPIKE'S WOUNDS.

Sally and Martha had made a big pot of chicken broth, and we now tried to feed some to Spike, but failed in our attempt. The smell of the broth didn't wake him, and the taste of it on his tongue got no response, either. He was unconscious and I knew that without food and water, he could not live.

Jack said, "I once had a dog that got a snakebite on the tongue and couldn't eat, and I had to devise a way to force-feed him until the swelling went down. I used a hollow, flexible tube. That's what we need now. Do you have one?"

We all started looking for something hollow and flexible that we could use to force-feed Spike. The only thing we could find that would fit the bill was an enema bottle. Sally washed it and the tube with hot soapy water and then disinfected it with alcohol.

The task ahead was going to be very tricky. I was to push the tube down Spike's throat and into his stomach, being very careful not to let the tube get into his windpipe. If that happened, the broth would drown him.

I started threading the tube down Spike's throat and couldn't tell if it was in the right place or not. Jack said, "If you'd like, I'll do it." I handed him the bottle and tube and he began working with it. After a couple of minutes, he said, "I think it's in the right place."

"ARE YOU SURE?" I ASKED.

HE SAID, "I CAN'T BE ABSOLUTELY CERTAIN, BUT I'M ABOUT AS SURE AS ONE CAN BE."

I SAID, "OK," AND HELD THE BLADDER UP WHILE SALLY SLOWLY POURED A PINT OF WARM BROTH INTO IT. THE BROTH INSTANTLY RAN THROUGH THE TUBE, AND WE KNEW THE TUBE WAS IN SPIKE'S STOMACH. WHEN THE BOTTLE WAS EMPTY, WE REMOVED THE TUBE, KNOWING THAT HIS FATE WAS NOW IN GOD'S HANDS.

WE STOOD AROUND THE TABLE, LOOKING AT SPIKE AND THINKING. HE WAS AS THIN AS A RAIL, AND WE KNEW THIS HAD TO HAVE HAPPENED THE DAY OF THE FIRE, IN ORDER FOR HIM TO HAVE LOST SO MUCH WEIGHT. WE MOVED HIM FROM THE HARD TABLE TO THE BOYS' BED.

SALLY SAT ON THE EDGE OF THE BED FOR SEVERAL HOURS, GENTLY RUBBING HIS HEAD, BEGGING, "SPIKE, PLEASE DON'T DIE. PLEASE, GOD, LET SPIKE LIVE. YOU HAVE MY TWO SONS, SO PLEASE GRANT ME THIS ONE THING."

LATE IN THE NIGHT, SALLY FINALLY FELL ASLEEP, LYING ON THE BED BESIDE SPIKE WITH HER HAND ON HIS HEAD. I PICKED HER UP AND PUT HER ON OUR BED, THEN CHECKED SPIKE; HE WAS BARELY ALIVE.

JACK AND MARTHA BEDDED DOWN IN THE FRONT ROOM AND I LAY DOWN WITH SALLY. I WAS UNABLE TO SLEEP. I HAD TOLD SALLY THAT SPIKE BEING ALIVE IN NO WAY MEANT THERE WAS HOPE THAT THE CHILDREN

COULD BE ALIVE, BUT, DOWN DEEP, I FELT THAT MAYBE THEY COULD BE. I KNEW SPIKE WOULD NEVER LEAVE THE BOYS; BUT IF THEY DID ESCAPE THE FIERY INFERNO AT THE SCHOOL, WHERE COULD THEY BE? I CONVINCED MYSELF THAT THE POSSIBILITY OF THEM BEING ALIVE WAS JUST WISHFUL THINKING ON MY PART. THERE WAS NO WAY THEY COULD BE ALIVE.

I DON'T KNOW WHAT IT WAS, BUT SOMETHING JUST WOULDN'T LET ME ACCEPT THIS LINE OF REASONING, AND I LAY THERE ALL NIGHT, TOSSING THINGS BACK AND FORTH IN MY MIND, TRYING TO MAKE SOME SENSE OUT OF IT. I FINALLY DECIDED THAT, COME MORNING, I WAS GOING TO HAVE TO GO OUT AGAIN AND SEARCH FOR ANY KIND OF SIGN IN THE DIRECTION THAT SPIKE HAD COME FROM.

AT LONG LAST, DAYLIGHT STARTED CREEPING THROUGH THE BEDROOM WINDOW, SO I GOT UP AND CHECKED ON SPIKE. HIS HEARTBEAT WAS STILL VERY FAINT. I COULDN'T TELL ANY DIFFERENCE FROM THE NIGHT BEFORE. I STILL DIDN'T HOLD MUCH HOPE FOR HIS RECOVERY.

MARTHA WAS ALREADY UP AND HAD BREAKFAST STARTED. I PITCHED IN AND HELPED HER SO SALLY COULD SLEEP. IT WAS THE FIRST TIME SALLY HAD SLEPT SINCE THE FIRE, AND I KNEW SHE WAS EXHAUSTED. WE HAD BREAKFAST ON THE TABLE WHEN SHE WALKED IN.

MARTHA KNEW HOW TO MAKE SALLY'S DAY. SHE HAD MADE SOME JELLY ROLLS JUST THE WAY SALLY LIKED THEM, AND HAD FIXED HASHBROWNS, SCRAMBLED

EGGS AND A PAN OF SOURMILK BISCUITS. THIS WAS SALLY'S FAVORITE MEAL, AND A SMILE CAME TO HER FACE AS SHE WALKED OVER AND PUT HER ARMS AROUND HER MOTHER AND KISSED HER ON THE CHEEK.

AFTER WE'D FINISHED BREAKFAST, JACK AND I WENT TO THE BARN TO DO THE CHORES. I SAID, "JACK, AFTER WE GET THE CHORES DONE, I'M GOING OUT AGAIN TO SEARCH FOR SIGNS THAT MIGHT LEAD US TO WHERE SPIKE WAS ATTACKED."

JACK SAID, "I'D LIKE TO GO WITH YOU."

SO, WHEN WE FINISHED WITH THE CHORES, WE WENT TO THE HOUSE AND TOLD MARTHA AND SALLY OF OUR PLAN. SALLY SAID, "CHECK SPIKE AGAIN BEFORE YOU LEAVE."

I SAID, "I CHECKED HIM EARLIER WHEN I FIRST GOT UP," BUT SHE INSISTED THAT I CHECK HIM AGAIN. I CHECKED HIM AND COULD SEE THAT THERE WAS NO CHANGE. HIS HEARTBEAT WAS STILL WEAK, AND HE DIDN'T RESPOND TO MY TOUCH OR MY VOICE. I TRIED TOUCHING HIS EYELID WITH MY FINGER, FIGURING THAT IF HE WAS CONSCIOUS HE WOULD RESPOND BY TWITCHING HIS EYE. I EVEN CLAPPED MY HANDS, HOPING THE SOUND WOULD CAUSE SOME RESPONSE, BUT AGAIN, NOTHING.

I SAID, "JACK, BEFORE WE LEAVE, I THINK WE SHOULD FORCE-FEED SPIKE AGAIN." HE AGREED, AND SALLY BEGAN WARMING UP THE BROTH. WE DISINFECTED THE BOTTLE AND TUBE AND BEGAN THREADING IT DOWN SPIKE'S THROAT. THIS TIME, IT WORKED MUCH BETTER, AND WE GAVE HIM ANOTHER PINT OF WARM BROTH.

I said, "If Spike lives for the next twenty-four hours without infection setting in, he might possibly make it; but right now, I don't hold much hope for him."

Jack and I had cleaned the deep wounds as good as we could. All the stitches were good and tight, and there was no evidence of bleeding, but just to be on the safe side, we took some boric acid and applied it gently to all the wounds. We knew the boric acid would help keep down the threat of infection. After the stitches were dry, we covered him up so he'd stay warm. I was afraid he might die from shock, and I knew the warmer we could keep him, the better his chances would be.

Jack and I put on our coats, and as I reached for my rifle, I said, "That's all we can do for Spike now, Sally. We're going to look for signs that might lead us to where he was attacked."

As we started out the door, Sally squeezed my hand, and she and Martha wished us luck.

SEVEN

UNCONSCIOUS, BUT ALIVE

THE AIR IN THE CAVE WAS GETTING STALE. THEY HAD BEEN TRAPPED IN THE CAVE FOR TWO DAYS WITHOUT FOOD. AND THE ONLY WATER THEY'D HAD TO DRINK WAS WHEN JIMMY HAD FELT WATER DRIPPING FROM THE CEILING OF THE CAVE IN SEVERAL PLACES AND HAD HAD ALL THE KIDS TAKE TURNS LYING ON THE GROUND UNDER THE DRIPS, HOLDING THEIR MOUTHS OPEN TO CATCH THE DROPS OF WATER. IT WAS LIKE A GAME TO THEM. EVEN THOUGH THEY WERE HUNGRY AND THIRSTY, THEY KNEW SPIKE WOULD SOON BRING HELP.

IT WAS DARK IN THE CAVE, AND THE SMALLER CHILDREN WERE CRYING -- BOTH FROM BEING AFRAID OF THE DARK AND FROM HUNGER. THERE WAS NOTHING ANY-ONE COULD DO EXCEPT TRY AND COMFORT ONE ANOTHER. MRS. MILLER WAS TRYING TO KEEP THEM CALM BY TELL-ING THEM STORIES. SHE TOLD THEM THE ENTIRE STORY OF EVERY BOOK SHE'D EVER READ.

SOME OF THE CHILDREN BELIEVED THEY'D BEEN TRAPPED IN THE CAVE FOR A WEEK, BUT MRS. MILLER AND JIMMY TOLD THEM IT HAD ONLY BEEN A COUPLE OF DAYS SINCE THE CAVE HAD BEEN SEALED BY THE TREACHEROUS STORM.

JIMMY KNEW SOMETHING WAS WRONG. SPIKE

73

SHOULD HAVE RETURNED WITH HELP BEFORE NOW. HE DECIDED THAT THEIR ONLY HOPE WAS TO TRY ONCE MORE TO DIG THEIR WAY OUT, SO HE STARTED MOVING ROCKS AND TOLD THE OTHERS TO STAY BACK. AFTER ONLY A COUPLE OF MINUTES, SOME OF THE LOOSE ROCKS WERE ALREADY ROLLING TOWARD THE INSIDE OF THE CAVE.

THE TUNNEL JIMMY WAS MAKING KEPT CAVING IN WITH LOOSE ROCK FROM ABOVE, BUT HE WOULDN'T QUIT. AFTER A COUPLE OF HOURS, HE SAW LIGHT. HE HAD MADE A SMALL OPENING TO THE OUTSIDE, AND AS HE MOVED HIS HEAD CLOSE TO THE HOLE TO LOOK OUT, HE FELT FRESH AIR FLOWING INTO THE CAVE, HITTING HIS FACE. THIS MEANT THAT THERE HAD TO BE ANOTHER OPENING TO THE CAVE. HE HURRIED TO THE TEACHER AND TOLD HER AND THE CHILDREN WHAT HE HAD DISCOV-ERED. HE SAID, "I'M GOING TO TRY AND FIND THE OTHER OPENING."

EVERYONE WAS EXCITED NOW, BUT THEY WERE STILL SCARED. THEY KNEW IF JIMMY COULDN'T FIND A WAY OUT, THEY WERE DOOMED.

THE LIGHT FROM THE HOLE JIMMY HAD MADE LET IN ONLY ENOUGH LIGHT TO MAKE OUT OUTLINES NEAR THE FRONT OF THE CAVE, AND AS HE MADE HIS WAY BACK INTO THE CAVE, HE HAD TO FEEL HIS WAY ALONG.

HE STARTED DOWN THE LEFT WALL, EXPLORING THE ENTIRE WALL WITH HIS HANDS, TRYING TO FIND AN OPENING. HE WENT FARTHER BACK INTO THE CAVE, REACHING AS HIGH AS HE COULD REACH, COVERING EVERY SQUARE INCH OF THE CAVE WALLS BY MOVING HIS HANDS.

He was about thirty feet back inside the cave before he found another opening. It was so small, he could barely get his head through it and could feel no air movement. He knew this wasn't the opening he was looking for, so he kept searching, knowing that his finding the other entrance was their only hope.

Jimmy's hands were getting sore. The sharp, jagged rocks on the cave wall were like sandpaper. His hands were bleeding, but he refused to stop. He found more small openings, but there was no air movement through them.

Finally, he came to what he thought was the end of the cave. There was a small opening, and as he felt the wall, it felt like it went back toward the entrance. He tried to squeeze through the small opening, and suddenly knew he was on the right track! He felt a light flow of air across his face and realized that it wasn't the end of the cave at all.

After he had squeezed through to the other side, he was feeling his way along and felt the cave widen. He then realized that it was getting lighter; that meant he was near the other entrance. He was getting excited now, and as the cave wall curved slightly to the right, a small light appeared, shining on the floor directly in front of him. He looked up and saw a crevasse about a foot long and no more than four inches wide -- about eight feet straight up.

JIMMY STOOD THERE LOOKING UP. HE KNEW THERE WAS NO WAY TO GET TO THE CREVASSE, AND EVEN IF HE DID, HE COULDN'T GET THROUGH IT; IT WAS FAR TOO SMALL. HIS HANDS WERE THROBBING WITH PAIN, AND AS HE HELD THEM UP TO THE LIGHT, HE SAW THAT THEY WERE RED WITH BLOOD. HE KNELT DOWN ON THE FLOOR OF THE CAVE, DIRECTLY UNDER THE SMALL RAY OF LIGHT, AND PUTTING HIS BLEEDING PALMS TOGETHER, PLACED THEM AGAINST HIS CHIN. HE LOOKED UP AT THE LIGHT AND SAID THE LORD'S PRAYER.

WEAK FROM HUNGER AND EXHAUSTED FROM EXERTION, WITH THEIR LAST HOPE NOW GONE, JIMMY LAY DOWN ON THE FLOOR OF THE CAVE AND FELL ASLEEP.

AT THE FARM, JACK AND I WENT TO THE SPOT WHERE WE'D FOUND SPIKE. WE FOUND HIS TRACKS; THEY WERE COMING FROM THE DIRECTION OF THE CREEK. THE GROUND WAS STILL WET, AND THE TRACKS WERE FAIRLY EASY TO FOLLOW AT FIRST; THEN WE GOT INTO SOME HEAVY UNDERBRUSH AND LOST THE TRAIL.

WE DECIDED TO GO ON PAST THE DENSE BRUSH AND TRY AND PICK UP THE TRAIL ON THE OTHER SIDE. WE SEARCHED FOR A LONG TIME, TO NO AVAIL. WE COULD FIND NO SIGNS. WE SLOWLY WORKED OUR WAY FARTHER OUT, AND AFTER AN HOUR OR SO, WE FOUND A SPOT IN THE LEAVES WHERE SOMETHING HAD BEEN LAYING. WE NOTICED SEVERAL DROPS OF BLOOD. I SAID, "JACK, IT LOOKS LIKE WE'RE ON THE RIGHT TRACK."

NOW THERE WAS A PROBLEM; THE LEAVES WERE SO THICK, WE COULDN'T FOLLOW THE TRAIL. AS WE CONTINUED OUR SEARCH, WE FOUND DROPS OF BLOOD

EVERY ONCE IN AWHILE. THIS WAS THE ONLY SIGN WE COULD FIND. THE DROPS OF BLOOD WERE LEADING US IN THE GENERAL DIRECTION OF THE CREEK.

THE SMALL BRANCH JUST NORTH OF THE HOUSE RAN WEST FOR A HALF MILE AND THEN RAN INTO THE ILLINOIS RIVER, WHICH RAN SOUTH. AT THIS POINT, THE RIVER WAS NOT VERY BIG, AND WE REFERRED TO IT AS A CREEK. THIS SEEMED TO BE WHERE SPIKE'S TRAIL WAS COMING FROM.

BY MID-AFTERNOON, WE'D FOUND NOTHING NEW. WE DECIDED TO GO BACK TO THE HOUSE FOR SOMETHING TO EAT AND DRINK; THEN WE'D COME BACK AND TRY AGAIN. WE WERE ABOUT A MILE FROM THE HOUSE AND THE CREEK WAS STILL ABOUT A MILE AWAY IF WE CONTINUED IN THE SAME DIRECTION. IF WE TURNED BACK MORE WEST, IT WAS ONLY A SHORT DISTANCE TO THE CREEK, BUT THAT WASN'T THE DIRECTION SPIKE HAD COME FROM.

QUESTIONS KEPT COMING TO MY MIND. WHY WOULD SPIKE BE THIS FAR FROM THE SCHOOL? DID HE LEAVE THE SCHOOL TO VISIT HIS FAMILY IN THE WILD?

ALL THE WAY BACK TO THE CABIN, NEITHER JACK NOR I HAD ANYTHING TO SAY. WE WERE BOTH THINKING ABOUT WHAT WE SHOULD DO NEXT.

WHEN WE GOT TO THE HOUSE, WE TOLD SALLY AND MARTHA WHAT WE HAD FOUND. I SAID, "SALLY, AS SOON AS WE GET A BITE TO EAT WE'RE GOING ON OVER TO THE CREEK AND SEE WHAT WE CAN FIND THERE."

SALLY AND HER MOTHER HAD FIXED DINNER EARLIER, AND IT WAS STILL HOT ON THE STOVE. THEY

HAD COOKED A POT OF BEANS AND HAD MADE A BIG PAN OF CRACKLING CORNBREAD. JACK AND I ATE OUR FILL, THEN SAT BACK AND RELAXED FOR A FEW MINUTES WHILE LAYING OUT OUR PLAN OVER A CUP OF COFFEE. JACK REMEMBERED THAT THERE WERE A FEW SMALL CAVES ALONG THE CREEK AND FIGURED THAT MIGHT BE A GOOD PLACE TO START LOOKING. HE THOUGHT THE CAVES WOULD ALSO BE A GOOD PLACE FOR A BEAR'S DEN.

I'D NEVER SEEN BUT ONE OR TWO BEARS EACH YEAR, AND THEY WERE AFRAID OF PEOPLE. THEN, ALL OF A SUDDEN, IT HIT ME LIKE A ROCK! IF THE KIDS MADE IT OUT OF THE SCHOOLHOUSE AND HEADED DOWN-STREAM TO GET AWAY FROM THE FIRE, THEY MIGHT HAVE FOUND SHELTER IN A CAVE; AND AFTER GOING INTO THE CAVE, A BEAR COULD HAVE COME IN AND GOTTEN INTO A FIGHT WITH SPIKE. MAYBE THE KIDS HAD GONE WAY BACK INTO THE CAVE TO GET AS FAR AWAY FROM THE BEAR AS THEY COULD, AND AFTER SPIKE GOT AWAY FROM THE BEAR, IT STAYED IN THE CAVE, AND THE KIDS COULDN'T GET OUT. IT MADE SENSE TO ME!

I COULDN'T WAIT TO GET JACK OUTSIDE TO TELL HIM WHAT I'D THOUGHT OF! I DIDN'T WANT TO SAY ANYTHING IN FRONT OF SALLY. I DIDN'T WANT TO GET HER HOPES UP. I FELT A LETDOWN WOULD MAKE IT JUST THAT MUCH HARDER ON HER.

WHEN JACK AND I GOT OUTSIDE, I TOLD HIM WHAT I HAD THOUGHT OF. I SAID, "JACK, DO YOU THINK IT MIGHT BE POSSIBLE FOR SOMETHING LIKE THAT TO HAVE HAPPENED?"

HE THOUGHT IT WAS INDEED POSSIBLE, SO WE

HEADED STRAIGHT FOR THE CREEK. WHEN WE GOT
THERE, WE SAW BLUFFS ON EACH SIDE OF IT. WE
SEARCHED BOTH SIDES AS WE WENT ALONG FOR ANY SIGN
THAT MIGHT LEAD US TO THE KIDS. WE SAW SEVERAL
CAVES, BUT WE DIDN'T HAVE A LANTERN WITH US. WE
FOUND NOTHING, SO NEAR SUNDOWN, WE DECIDED TO CALL
IT A DAY AND HEADED FOR THE FARM.

THE ELECTRICAL STORM THAT HAD CAUSED THE
TRAGEDY WAS THE WORST ELECTRICAL STORM I HAD EVER
SEEN. ON THE WAY HOME THAT AFTERNOON, WE SAW
SEVERAL TREES THAT HAD BEEN STRUCK BY LIGHTNING.
ONE OF THEM, A GIANT OAK, ABOUT THREE FEET
THROUGH, HAD BEEN REDUCED TO KINDLING. IT LOOKED
LIKE SOMEONE HAD SET OFF DYNAMITE AND BLOWN THE
TREE TO BITS.

IT WAS ALMOST DARK AS WE NEARED THE HOUSE.
I SAID, "JACK, IT LOOKS AS IF I'LL BE CHORING BY
THE LIGHT OF THE LANTERN AGAIN."

HE SAID, "I'LL LEND A HAND AND IT WON'T
TAKE LONG."

AS WE WALKED THROUGH THE DOOR, SALLY AND
MARTHA SAID, "HURRY AND TELL US WHAT YOU FOUND."

THEY WERE REALLY DISAPPOINTED WHEN WE TOLD
THEM WE HADN'T FOUND ANYTHING. SALLY SAID,
"PLEASE LOOK AGAIN TOMORROW." I ASSURED HER WE
WOULD.

I CHECKED SPIKE AND COULD SEE NO CHANGE.
I SAID, "SALLY, AFTER WE GET FINISHED WITH THE
CHORES, WE'LL NEED TO FORCE-FEED SPIKE AGAIN.
WILL YOU MAKE READY SOME BROTH?" SALLY SAID

SHE'D HAVE EVERYTHING READY, SO I GOT THE MILK BUCKET, AND JACK AND I HEADED FOR THE BARN.

BOTH COWS WERE LYING IN FRONT OF THE BARN. I FIGURED THEY WERE WONDERING WHAT HAD HAPPENED TO THEIR SCHEDULE. AS I OPENED THE DOOR AND PICKED UP THE LANTERN TO LIGHT, THE COWS PUSHED THEIR WAY IN, WANTING THEIR GRAIN. I GAVE EACH ONE A HARDY HELPING, THEN SAT DOWN ON THE STOOL AND STARTED MILKING.

JACK SAID, "IF YOU CAN MILK IN THE DARK, I'LL TAKE THE LANTERN AND GATHER THE EGGS AND FEED THE PIGS."

"GO AHEAD AND TAKE IT," I SAID. "I'VE MILKED IN THE DARK MANY TIMES. BESIDES, I CAN THINK BETTER IN THE DARK." I FINISHED MILKING BELL, AND AS I FELT MY WAY OVER TO ROSE, I THOUGHT ABOUT HOW MUCH PEOPLE RELY ON OTHER SENSES IN THE DARK. I FOUND MYSELF USING MY HANDS AND FEET TO FEEL MY WAY AROUND THE BARN. I LOCATED ROSE, THEN TOOK UP THE MILKING POSITION AND WENT TO WORK. I WAS ABOUT HALF THROUGH WHEN JACK CAME BACK WITH THE LANTERN.

I LOOKED UP AND SAID, "JACK, I CAN'T QUIT SEARCHING THE CREEK TILL I'M SATISFIED THERE'S NOTHING THERE."

HE SAID, "I FEEL THE SAME WAY."

AFTER I FINISHED THE MILKING, I PUT THE COWS IN THE CORRAL, AND WE TOOK THE MILK AND EGGS TO THE HOUSE.

SALLY HAD THE BROTH WARM AND THE BOTTLE

AND TUBE CLEANED AND DISINFECTED, SO JACK AND I FORCE-FED SPIKE AND CHECKED FOR REFLEXES. THERE WERE NONE. WE CLEANED HIS WOUNDS AGAIN WITH BORIC ACID, THEN COVERED HIM BACK UP.

WHILE WE WERE EATING SUPPER, JACK AND I TALKED ABOUT THE ILLINOIS RIVER AND HOW THE HEAD OF IT IS A HALF MILE OR SO NORTH OF HERE AND A MILE SOUTH. SOME OF THE BLUFFS CUT BY TIME ARE THIRTY AND FORTY FEET HIGH. JACK NOTED THAT THE WATER IN THIS PART OF THE COUNTRY IS SPARKLING CLEAR AND HAS A VERY SWEET TASTE, AND THERE ARE MANY SPRINGS ALONG THE CREEK THAT RUN YEAR ROUND, EVEN DURING THE DRIEST PART OF SUMMER.

I SAID, "THIS COUNTRY HAS BEEN BLESSED WITH RICH, FERTILE SOIL AND PLENTY OF WATER. THE ONLY THINGS I DON'T LIKE ABOUT THIS COUNTRY ARE THE COPPERHEAD SNAKES."

JACK SAID, "I DON'T CARE MUCH FOR THEM EITHER, BUT I GUESS EVERY PLACE A FELLOW COULD FIND TO LIVE WOULD HAVE SOMETHING HE'D LIKE TO HAVE CHANGED."

THE REST OF THE EVENING WAS SPENT WITH SMALL TALK ABOUT FIRST ONE THING AND THEN ANOTHER.

THE NEXT MORNING AT FIRST LIGHT, I CHECKED SPIKE. HIS HEARTBEAT WAS A LITTLE STRONGER, OR AT LEAST IT SEEMED TO BE.

WE ATE BREAKFAST, THEN, WHILE I DID THE CHORES, SALLY PREPARED THINGS FOR FORCE-FEEDING SPIKE.

WHEN WE STARTED THREADING THE TUBE DOWN

81

SPIKE'S THROAT, HE GAGGED AND WE KNEW IT WAS A GOOD SIGN. WE FINALLY GOT HIM FED, AND SALLY SAT THERE STROKING HIS HEAD AS JACK AND I WALKED OUT THE DOOR.

WE STOPPED BY THE BARN TO GET THE LANTERN, THEN FILLED IT WITH COAL OIL SO WE COULD SEARCH THE CAVES WE HAD SEEN THE DAY BEFORE. WE HEADED TO THE CREEK TO TAKE UP WHERE WE HAD LEFT OFF YESTERDAY.

WHEN WE GOT TO THE CREEK AND RESUMED OUR SEARCH, WE FOUND MANY CREVASSES IN THE BLUFFS, BUT NONE LARGE ENOUGH NOR DEEP ENOUGH FOR ANYONE TO HIDE IN. TOWARD LATE MORNING, WE FOUND A LARGE AREA COVERED WITH BLOOD AND TRACKS LEADING AWAY. THE TRACKS WERE SPIKE'S.

WE STARTED SEARCHING FOR A CAVE NEARBY, BUT COULD FIND NOTHING, SO WE WENT DOWNSTREAM AWAYS WHERE WE FOUND A SMALL CAVE. WE LIT THE LANTERN AND WENT INSIDE. IT WAS VERY SMALL AND DIDN'T TAKE LONG TO SEARCH. WE FOUND NO SIGNS OF A FIGHT AND NO FOOTPRINTS OF ANY KIND ON THE CAVE FLOOR.

WE KNEW THE FIGHT BETWEEN SPIKE AND THE BEAR HAD TO HAVE TAKEN PLACE NEAR HERE. WOUNDED THE WAY SPIKE WAS, HE COULDN'T HAVE TRAVELED FAR WITHOUT LYING DOWN, AND WE KNEW THE BLOODY AREA WE'D FOUND WAS WHERE HE HAD LAY FOR A LONG TIME. WE ALSO KNEW HE WAS LYING THERE DURING THE RAIN BECAUSE SOME OF THE BLOOD HAD BEEN DILUTED BY THE WATER AND HAD STAINED THE GROUND.

WHEN WE LEFT THE SMALL CAVE AND HEADED DOWNSTREAM, WE NOTICED A LARGE ROCKSLIDE ON THE OTHER SIDE OF THE CREEK. WE COULD TELL IT HAD BEEN CAUSED BY THE STORM, BECAUSE IN THE MIDDLE OF THE SLIDE WAS A BIG OAK TREE THAT HAD BEEN SHATTERED BY THE LIGHTNING. THERE WERE SOME VERY LARGE BOULDERS IN THE SLIDE.

AFTER A TIME, WE SAW ANOTHER CAVE AND APPROACHED WITH CAUTION, THINKING THE BEAR MIGHT BE INSIDE; BUT WHEN WE GOT TO THE ENTRANCE, WE FOUND NO TRACKS. WE SEARCHED THE CAVE ANYHOW. IT TOOK ABOUT THIRTY MINUTES. WE COULDN'T FIND A THING.

BY NOW, IT WAS DINNERTIME, AND SINCE WE HAD BROUGHT SOME DRIED MEAT ALONG, WE DECIDED TO STAY OUT ALL DAY AND COMPLETE OUR SEARCH. WE SAT DOWN AT THE ENTRANCE OF THE CAVE AND ATE SOME OF THE MEAT. WE TALKED FOR A SPELL AND FIGURED THAT IF WE DIDN'T FIND ANYTHING IN THE NEXT MILE, WE'D BE WASTING OUR TIME. AFTER A BRIEF REST, WE CONTINUED OUR QUEST, BUT TO NO AVAIL. WE FOUND ONLY A COUPLE OF SMALL CAVES, AND THERE WAS NO SIGN OF ANYTHING IN EITHER OF THEM.

IT WAS NOW LATE AFTERNOON, AND WE KNEW THE NEWS WE WOULD BE TAKING HOME WOULD DISSOLVE THAT TINY BIT OF HOPE, BUT WE HAD NO CHOICE BUT TO RETURN HOME EMPTY-HANDED.

ON THE WAY HOME I ASKED, "JACK, HOW LONG WILL YOU AND MARTHA BE STAYING?"

HE SAID, "I FIGURE WE'LL BE STAYING FOR A COUPLE OR THREE MORE DAYS, SINCE MARTHA FEELS THAT

SHE NEEDS TO BE WITH SALLY FOR AT LEAST THAT
LONG."

"WHO'S TENDING TO YOUR THINGS AT HOME?"
I ASKED.

HE SAID, "PAUL, IS WATCHING AFTER THINGS
FOR US." PAUL, SALLY'S YOUNGER BROTHER LIVED JUST
A SHORT DISTANCE AWAY.

THE SUN WAS STILL UP WHEN WE GOT TO THE
HOUSE. WE TOLD SALLY AND MARTHA WHAT WE HAD
FOUND. THEY WERE BOTH DISAPPOINTED, AND YET RE-
LIEVED IN A WAY. THERE WAS NOTHING TO DO NOW
BUT GO ON.

MARTHA AND JACK TRIED COMFORTING SALLY THE
REST OF THE DAY BY SAYING, "SALLY, THE BEST THING
TO DO IS TO HAVE MORE CHILDREN. WE KNOW YOU'RE
A GOOD CHRISTIAN AND BELIEVE IN GOD, AND YOU KNOW
THE BOYS WILL BE WAITING FOR YOU WHEN YOUR TIME
COMES TO LEAVE THIS OLD WORLD."

SALLY SAID, "I KNOW ALL THAT, BUT IT DOES-
N'T MAKE IT ANY EASIER."

WE WERE RUNNING LOW ON SUPPLIES, SO JACK
AND I DECIDED TO GO INTO TOWN THE NEXT DAY AND
STOCK UP. SALLY AND MARTHA STARTED MAKING OUT A
LIST OF WHAT WAS NEEDED FOR THE HOUSE.

JACK AND I WERE SITTING AT THE TABLE
DRINKING A CUP OF COFFEE AND TALKING ABOUT FIRST
ONE THING AND THEN ANOTHER. WE HEARD A WHINING
SOUND AND STOPPED TALKING. WE HELD SILENT, BUT
DIDN'T HEAR ANYTHING ELSE. JACK ASKED, "WHAT WAS
THAT NOISE?"

"I don't know," I answered, "probably the wind."

Satisfied with that, we resumed our conversation, but after a few minutes, we heard it again. We both got to our feet at the same time. Sally looked at us and asked, "Where are you going?"

Jack said, "Shhhh, listen." The room was totally silent as everyone listened. After a few seconds, we heard it again. The sound was coming from the bedroom, and we raced in to see what it was. Spike was awake and trying to get up.

Sally sat down on the edge of the bed and tried comforting him by rubbing his head; he always liked that. After a time, he relaxed and lay flat on his side. Sally said, "Watch him and don't let him move. I'll fix him some biscuits and gravy." That was Spike's favorite food.

While Sally was fixing him something to eat, he kept raising his head and whining. We knew he was in a lot of pain.

Finally, Sally brought in the biscuits and gravy. Spike must have been able to smell it, because he tried to sit up as she walked through the door. I helped him get into a position where he could eat.

Sally had broken the biscuits up into small pieces and had gravy over them. As I watched, I couldn't believe my eyes; she was feeding Spike out of one of her good pie pans! She had never

85

DONE THAT BEFORE! SHE PLACED THE PAN IN FRONT OF HIM, AND HE GOBBLED IT UP, THEN LICKED THE PAN CLEAN. WE COULD TELL THAT HE WANTED MORE, AND SALLY ASKED, "DO YOU THINK IT WOULD HURT TO GIVE HIM MORE?"

I SAID, "GO AHEAD AND GIVE HIM ABOUT HALF THAT MUCH MORE."

SALLY FED SPIKE MORE BISCUITS AND GRAVY, THEN BROUGHT HIM A BOWL OF WATER. HE DRANK A GOOD PORTION OF IT. SINCE SPIKE WAS CONSCIOUS AND HAD A GOOD APPETITE, I NOW THOUGHT HE MIGHT MAKE IT.

WE COULDN'T GET HIM TO LIE FLAT DOWN ON HIS SIDE. HE STRETCHED HIS BACK LEGS STRAIGHT OUT AND LAY ON HIS RIGHT HIP WITH HIS FRONT PAWS OUT IN FRONT OF HIM AND HIS HEAD LYING ON THEM. THIS IS THE WAY HE USUALLY LAY. NOW WITH HIM LYING PEACEFUL AND ALERT, SALLY WENT ABOUT FIXING SUPPER, AND I GOT THE MILK BUCKET AND WENT TO THE BARN.

I MADE A QUICK SURVEY TO SEE WHAT I NEEDED FROM TOWN AND THEN STARTED THE CHORES. WHEN I GOT BACK TO THE HOUSE, SUPPER WAS ALMOST READY, SO I POURED A CUP OF COFFEE, THEN SAT WITH JACK AT THE TABLE WHILE WE WAITED FOR SALLY TO FINISH SUPPER.

THE AIR OF SADNESS AND SORROW DIDN'T SEEM TO BE AS HEAVY AS IT HAD BEEN; THERE WASN'T AS MUCH TENSION. I THINK EVERYONE WAS RELIEVED AND HAPPY THAT AT LEAST SPIKE WAS GOING TO LIVE.

THE NEXT MORNING, SPIKE WAS MUCH BETTER. HE WAS WHINING AND TRYING TO GET OFF THE BED. IT LOOKED LIKE HE WOULD MAKE A FAST RECOVERY.

AFTER BREAKFAST AND FINISHING THE CHORES, I HARNESSED THE TEAM, THEN GOT SALLY'S LIST AND JACK AND I HEADED FOR TOWN. I SAID, "WE'LL GET BACK JUST AS SOON AS WE CAN, BUT DON'T LOOK FOR US TILL AROUND CHORE TIME." SALLY NODDED AND WAVED AS WE DROVE OFF.

Eight

Discovering the Cave

TOWN WAS A FIVE-MILE RIDE, AND IT TOOK A LITTLE OVER TWO HOURS TO GET THERE. WE COULD HAVE MADE IT SOONER, BUT WE STOPPED A COUPLE OF TIMES TO VISIT WITH SOME FRIENDS. ONCE IN TOWN, WE MADE THE USUAL ROUNDS BEFORE GATHERING UP THE SUPPLIES. MY USUAL ROUNDS INCLUDED VISITING WITH ALL THE STORE OWNERS TO CATCH UP ON THE LATEST NEWS. I ALSO CHECKED WITH THE HARDWARE STORE AND FEED MILL TO SEE WHAT WAS NEW IN THE FARM LINE.

THERE WERE THREE AUTOMOBILES IN TOWN THAT DAY. WHEN I FIRST HEARD ABOUT THEM SOME TIME BACK, I THOUGHT THEY MIGHT GO OVER IN THE BIG CITIES LIKE FT. SMITH, BUT UP HERE IN THE HILLS, I COULDN'T SEE ANYONE IN THEIR RIGHT MIND EVER WANTING ONE; NOW I'M BEGINNING TO WONDER. I NEVER THOUGHT I'D EVER SEE ONE IN THIS TOWN, BUT HERE THEY WERE. JACK AND I LOOKED THEM OVER REAL GOOD AND ALLOWED IT'D BE A LONG TIME BEFORE WE EVER TOOK ONE HOME.

WE GATHERED UP OUR SUPPLIES AND HEADED HOME, KNOWING THAT BY THE TIME WE GOT BACK IT'D BE CHORE TIME. WE HAD SPENT MORE TIME LOAFING THAN WE HAD INTENDED.

When we arrived home, the sun was setting fast. We carried the supplies Sally wanted into the house, and when we walked through the door, I was surprised to see Spike standing there.

Sally said, "Spike got off the bed right after dinner, and he's been wanting out ever since. He keeps scratching at the door. I was afraid to let him out, afraid he might hurt himself."

I said, "I agree. He should stay in for a few more days. We'll have to watch him closely when we do let him out." When I opened the door to go out, it was all I could do to keep Spike inside. He sure wanted outside, bad.

I went on to the barn and took the harness off the horses, then gave them a scoop of oats and continued with the rest of the chores. After choring, while I was straining the milk, I realized that we had accumulated a lot of cream, and I thought that after supper I'd churn out the cream and make butter and some good buttermilk, for cooking as well as drinking. I could make a meal out of buttermilk and crackling cornbread.

I said, "Sally, I'm going to churn the cream after supper."

She said, "It'll be nice to have some fresh butter." So, while she finished preparing supper, I got out the churn and filled it with cream, then added a little salt. I always liked to add my salt before I churned. I knew that

90

MOST PEOPLE LIKED TO ADD SALT AFTER THE CHURNING WAS COMPLETED, BUT TO ME, IT'S JUST BETTER IF IT'S ADDED FIRST.

I WAS STILL ON THE PORCH GETTING THE CREAM READY TO CHURN WHEN SALLY ANNOUNCED SUPPER. I COULD FEEL A BRISK CHILL IN THE AIR, SO I CARRIED THE CHURN INSIDE AND SAT DOWN TO EAT.

AFTER SUPPER, I CHURNED THE CREAM WHILE SALLY AND MARTHA CLEANED THE KITCHEN. SALLY ASKED ME HOW MUCH BUTTER I WOULD HAVE, AND I TOLD HER I FIGURED ON THREE MOLDS FULL, SO SHE CLEANED THE MOLDS AND GOT THEM READY.

THE CREAM WAS A LITTLE COOL FOR FAST CHURNING, BUT IT WAS RIPE; IT SMELLED LIKE BLACK WALNUTS. THAT MEANT IT WOULD HAVE A FLAVOR JUST OUT OF THIS WORLD! IT TOOK ALMOST TWO HOURS BEFORE THE BUTTER STARTED TO BREAK. AFTER THAT, I HAD IT GATHERED, WORKED, SALTED, PRESSED AND IN THE MOLDS IN ABOUT AN HOUR. WE ALL HAD A LARGE GLASS OF BUTTERMILK, THEN I POURED THE REMAINDER INTO JARS AND SAT THEM ON THE BACK PORCH TO STAY COOL. IT WAS ABOUT THE BEST BUTTERMILK I HAD EVER DRANK.

WE SAT AT THE TABLE AND TALKED FOR AWHILE BEFORE TURNING IN. MARTHA SAID, "SALLY, I'LL HELP YOU GATHER UP JAKE'S AND TOM'S THINGS, AND WE'LL PUT THEM IN MOTH BALLS AND STORE THEM IN THE CLOSET UNTIL YOU'VE DECIDED WHAT TO DO WITH THEM."

I KNEW IT'D BE HARD TO DO, BUT WITH MARTHA HELPING, THEY COULD GET IT DONE BEFORE SHE LEFT.

91

She knew that the sooner it was done, the better it would be. Sally and I both knew she was right.

Martha said, "Jack, why don't you and Dave find something to do outside tomorrow."

I said, "I have some corn that needs to be harvested; Jack and I could work on that." On that note, we turned in for the night.

The next morning, Spike was whining and pawing at the door. I decided it best to let him out for a spell, and I opened the door. Spike, still unable to walk on all fours, hobbled off the porch and headed toward the woods. I kept thinking he would stop, but he kept right on going. I hollered at him. He paused and looked back at me, then yapped and continued on toward the woods. I yelled, "Jack, I may need your help!"

It was pretty chilly, so Jack grabbed his jacket as he ran out the door. Spike was now getting near the woods. He stopped and looked back, and as we started closing in on him, he turned and made his way into the woods, heading in the direction of the creek. I said, "Let's hurry, Jack; we need to catch him and carry him back to the house or he'll tear his wounds open."

I circled around in front of Spike in an attempt to catch him, and as I reached out to grab him, he stopped and growled ferociously at me, snarling and showing his teeth! I wondered

92

IF HE COULD HAVE RABIES; HE'D NEVER ACTED LIKE THIS BEFORE!

JACK SAID, "WE SHOULD JUST LET HIM GO AND FOLLOW HIM; LET HIM GET WHATEVER'S BOTHERING HIM OUT OF HIS SYSTEM."

I BACKED OFF AND SPIKE HEADED TOWARD THE CREEK WITH US RIGHT IN BEHIND HIM. HE DIDN'T STOP TILL HE GOT TO THE ROCKSLIDE THAT JACK AND I HAD SEEN. WHEN HE STOPPED, HE STARTED WHINING, GROWLING AND PAWING AT THE ROCKS WITH HIS RIGHT PAW. JACK AND I LOOKED AT EACH OTHER AND WITHOUT SAYING A WORD, WE STARTED MOVING ROCKS JUST AS FAST AS WE COULD! WE COULD TELL RIGHT OFF THAT WE WERE GOING ABOUT IT THE WRONG WAY, BECAUSE THE ROCKS ABOVE BEGAN TUMBLING DOWN. WE STOPPED AND TALKED FOR A MINUTE ABOUT WHAT WE SHOULD DO. WE THOUGHT WE HEARD A FAINT CRY. WE LISTENED CLOSELY AND HEARD THE SAME SOUND AGAIN. WE MOVED AROUND, TRYING TO PINPOINT THE SOURCE AND DISCOVERED THE SOUND WAS COMING FROM A SMALL HOLE IN THE MIDDLE OF THE ROCKSLIDE. AS I PUT MY HEAD CLOSE TO THE HOLE, I COULD HEAR KIDS CRYING AND HOLLERING. THEY HAD EVIDENTLY HEARD US MOVING THE ROCKS AND HAD STARTED YELLING, KNOWING SOMEONE WAS THERE.

JACK AND I WERE EXCITED NOW; WE KNEW WE'D FOUND THEM! I PUT MY MOUTH CLOSE TO THE HOLE AND YELLED, "GET BACK AWAY FROM THE ENTRANCE SO YOU WON'T GET HURT BY THE FALLING ROCKS."

I TURNED TO JACK AND SAID, "WE'RE GOING TO

HAVE TO HAVE HELP. SOME OF THESE LARGER BOULDERS CAN'T BE MOVED WITHOUT HORSES."

HE SAID, "I'LL GO FOR HELP," AND TOOK OFF IN A RUN.

I YELLED, "GO BY THE HOUSE AND TELL SALLY AND MARTHA THAT WE'VE FOUND THE KIDS. AND TELL THEM WE DON'T KNOW HOW MANY ARE STILL ALIVE, BUT WE CAN HEAR SEVERAL. THEY SHOULD FIX SOME FOOD -- WHATEVER THEY CAN FIND -- AND BRING IT. THEY'LL ALSO NEED TO BRING A KEG OF WATER. HURRY! THESE KIDS HAVE BEEN WITHOUT FOOD AND WATER FOR SIX DAYS!"

I AGAIN PUT MY MOUTH NEAR THE HOLE AND TRIED TALKING TO THE KIDS. I HOLLERED, "IS EVERYONE ALL RIGHT?" I LISTENED. ALL I COULD HEAR WAS FAINT SCREAMING AND YELLING. I MADE SEVERAL ATTEMPTS TO GET SOME IDEA OF HOW MANY WERE THERE AND HOW THEY WERE DOING, BUT EVERYONE WAS HYSTERICAL, AND I COULDN'T MAKE SENSE OUT OF ANYTHING THEY WERE SAYING. I TRIED SEVERAL TIMES TO ASSURE THEM THAT WE'D HAVE THEM OUT IN JUST A LITTLE WHILE.

I BEGAN MOVING THE ROCKS I COULD HANDLE. I KNEW WE'D NEED CHOPPING AXES BECAUSE THERE WERE BIG TREES INTERMINGLED IN THE ROCKSLIDE. I WASN'T MAKING MUCH HEADWAY; THERE WASN'T MUCH I COULD DO WITHOUT HELP, BUT I COULDN'T JUST SIT THERE AND DO NOTHING.

I WAS AS ANXIOUS AS I COULD BE. IT SEEMED AS THOUGH JACK HAD BEEN GONE FOR A LONG TIME, BUT

I KNEW HE'D ONLY BEEN GONE FOR A LITTLE WHILE.

IT'S IMPOSSIBLE TO EXPLAIN HOW I FELT. I HAD THOUGHT MY TWO SONS WERE DEAD. FUNERAL SERVICES HAD BEEN HELD FOR THEM, AND NOW IT SEEMED AS THOUGH THEY MIGHT BE ALIVE. I DIDN'T KNOW FOR SURE; ALL I KNEW WAS THAT SEVERAL OF THE KIDS WERE ALIVE. BUT WHICH ONES? I HAD NO WAY OF KNOWING. I KNEW THEY'D BEEN TRAPPED FOR SIX DAYS, AND IN SIX DAYS, SMALL CHILDREN COULD STARVE TO DEATH.

I MOVED ALL THE ROCKS I COULD. KNOWING THE GIANT BOULDERS WOULD HAVE TO BE MOVED NEXT, I MADE MY WAY BACK TO WHERE THE SMALL OPENING WAS, BUT IT HAD BEEN SEALED BY THE SETTLING ROCKS. I TRIED CALLING TO THE KIDS, OVER AND OVER, BUT I GOT NO RESPONSE. THERE WAS NOTHING I COULD DO NOW BUT WAIT FOR HELP.

THERE WAS ONE GIANT BOULDER THAT WOULD HAVE TO BE MOVED BEFORE ANYTHING ELSE. IT WAS ABOUT TEN FEET WIDE AND FIFTEEN FEET TALL, AND THERE WAS NO WAY OF TELLING HOW THICK IT WAS. I FIGURED IT TO BE PART OF AN OVERHANGING OUTCROPPING THAT HAD BEEN DISLODGED BY THE LIGHTNING WHEN IT STRUCK THE TREE -- THE SAME TREE THAT WAS IN THE MIDDLE OF THE ROCKSLIDE.

I COULD NOW HEAR VOICES IN THE DISTANCE AND THE RATTLE OF CHAINS. I SAT THERE, NERVOUS AND ANXIOUSLY AWAITING THEIR ARRIVAL. IN A FEW MINUTES THEY CAME INTO VIEW; THERE WERE THREE MEN WITH TWO TEAMS.

I POINTED OUT THE PROBLEMS AS BEST I COULD. I SAID, "THE FIRST THING WE NEED TO DO IS PULL THAT BIG BOULDER OVER SOMEHOW SO WE CAN GET TO THE SMALLER ONES." I WAS AFRAID THAT IF WE TRIED TO MOVE MORE SMALL ONES, THE BIG ONE MIGHT SLIDE DOWN AND FALL TO THE INSIDE, CRUSHING THE CHILDREN. THEY ALL AGREED, BUT WEREN'T SURE JUST HOW WE'D BE ABLE TO MOVE SUCH A GIANT ROCK.

I SAID, "TAKE ALL THE CHAINS YOU HAVE AND ONE OF YOU GO AROUND AND CLIMB ON TOP OF THE BLUFF, THEN GET POSITIONED TO WHERE YOU CAN DROP THE CHAIN BEHIND THE TOP PART OF THE BIG ROCK."

SOMEONE SAID, "WE BROUGHT ALL THE CHAINS WE HAD, BUT THERE'S NOT ENOUGH FOR THAT."

"WE'LL JUST HAVE TO WORK WITH WHAT WE HAVE," I SAID, "TILL MORE ARRIVE."

MORE PEOPLE WERE SHOWING UP NOW, AND I NO-TICED THAT MOST OF THEM WERE PARENTS OF THE TRAPPED CHILDREN. VERY FEW HAD BROUGHT ANY TOOLS OR HORSES; MOST OF THEM HAD WALKED TO THE CREEK.

I SAW THE CHAOS AND CONFUSION THAT WAS GOING ON AND KNEW THAT SOMEONE WAS GOING TO HAVE TO TAKE CHARGE. I CALLED FOR EVERYONE'S ATTENTION AND EXPLAINED WHAT HAD HAPPENED -- HOW WE HAD FOUND THE CHILDREN AND WHAT HAD TO BE DONE NOW TO GET THEM OUT OF THE CAVE.

I SAID, "EVERYONE WHO HAS HORSES AT HOME SHOULD GO HOME, HARNESS THEM UP AND BRING THEM TO THE CREEK. BRING ALL THE CHAINS AND HEAVY ROPES YOU HAVE, AND IF YOU HAVE A BLOCK AND TACKLE,

BRING IT. THESE KIDS HAVE BEEN TRAPPED FOR SIX DAYS WITHOUT FOOD AND WATER AND WE HAVE TO GET THEM OUT. TELL EVERYONE YOU MEET ON THE WAY WHAT WE NEED, SO THEY CAN GO BACK HOME AND GET IT." THOSE WHO HADN'T BROUGHT HORSES TOOK OFF FOR HOME, STEPPING AT A BRISK PACE.

IT WAS SOME TIME BEFORE ANYONE ELSE SHOWED UP, BUT WHEN THEY DID, THEY HAD HORSES, CHAINS, BLOCKS AND TACKLE, AND ROPES; NOW, WE COULD GO TO WORK.

TWO OF THE MEN HAD MADE THEIR WAY TO THE TOP OF THE BLUFF WITH ROPES, AND THEY NOW DROPPED ONE END OF THE ROPE DOWN. WE TIED THE CHAINS TO IT AND AS THEY PULLED THE CHAINS UP, WE BEGAN TYING THE CHAINS TOGETHER. ONCE THEY GOT THE CHAINS TO THE TOP OF THE ROCK, THEY TRIED SLIP-PING IT BEHIND THE ROCK, USING THE ROPE AND SOME LIMBS THEY HAD TRIMMED FROM TREES. THEY WERE UNABLE TO GET THE CHAIN IN BEHIND THE ROCK FAR ENOUGH, AND AFTER A TIME, THEY DECIDED IT WAS NO USE.

RALPH CLIFTON, ONE OF THE MEN ON TOP OF THE BLUFF, HOLLERED DOWN, "SEND UP A COUPLE MORE MEN TO HELP LOWER ME DOWN, AND I'LL TRY AND GET THE CHAIN IN PLACE."

TWO MEN TOOK OFF UP THE CREEK TO FIND A WAY TO THE TOP OF THE BLUFF. ONCE ON TOP, THEY WERE ABLE TO ANCHOR THE ROPE AND LOWER RALPH SO THAT HE COULD PLACE THE CHAIN BEHIND THE ROCK. AFTER SEVERAL MINUTES, HE HOLLERED, "I'LL NEED A

HAMMER AND SOME KIND OF BAR TO KNOCK OUT A PLACE
IN THE CENTER OF THE ROCK SO I CAN GET THE CHAIN
DOWN FAR ENOUGH TO WORK."

THE MEN ON TOP TIED THE ROPE, WHICH WAS
HOLDING RALPH, TO A TREE. THEY LOWERED ANOTHER
ROPE TO THE CREEK BED WHERE WE TIED A HAMMER AND
BAR TO IT. THEY PULLED IT UP TO RALPH, AND HE
BEGAN HAMMERING AND POKING, TRYING TO GET THE
CHAIN INTO PLACE. AFTER SEVERAL MINUTES, RALPH
HOLLERED, "OK, I'VE GOT IT," AND THEY PULLED HIM
BACK TO THE TOP OF THE BLUFF.

EVERYONE DOWN BELOW RIGGED THE CHAINS AND
THEN HITCHED THE HORSES TO THEM, MAKING SURE THE
HORSES WERE HOOKED UP FAR ENOUGH AWAY FROM THE
ROCK THAT IT WOULDN'T FALL ON THEM AFTER IT
PASSED THE UPRIGHT POSITION. WE HITCHED TWO TEAMS
TO THE CHAINS, ONE ON EACH END. ONCE EVERYTHING
WAS SET AND EVERYONE WAS OUT OF THE WAY, THE
HORSES WERE SLAPPED WITH THE REINS AND A COMMAND
OF "GIT UP THERE!" WAS GIVEN. BOTH TEAMS PULLED
WITH FULL FORCE, BUT THE ROCK DIDN'T BUDGE. WE
TRIED AGAIN AND AGAIN, BUT IT WOULDN'T MOVE.

WE KNEW WE'D HAVE TO GATHER UP MORE CHAINS
AND HITCH EVEN MORE HORSES TO THEM. WE'D HAVE TO
RERIG THE WHOLE SETUP SO WE COULD HITCH EIGHT
HORSES TO THE ROCK; WE FELT THAT WOULD SURELY BE
ENOUGH.

ONCE THE TEAMS IN PLACE, ANOTHER ATTEMPT
WAS MADE TO MOVE THE ROCK. ON THE FIRST LUNGE,
THERE WAS NO MOVEMENT, THEN A SECOND ATTEMPT WAS

MADE; THE TOP OF THE ROCK MOVED SLIGHTLY AWAY FROM THE FACE OF THE BLUFF. THE HORSES TRIED HARD TO PULL THE ROCK AWAY, BUT THEY WERE BEGINNING TO WEAKEN, AND THE GIANT ROCK SETTLED BACK AGAINST THE FACE OF THE BLUFF. WE DECIDED TO LET THE HORSES REST FOR A FEW MINUTES BEFORE TRYING AGAIN.

AFTER A SHORT BREATHER, ANOTHER THRUST WAS MADE. THIS TIME, THE TOP OF THE ROCK MOVED A LITTLE FARTHER. IT CONTINUED TO MOVE SLOWLY UPWARD, NEARING THE UPRIGHT POSITION. WE COULD SEE THAT IT WOULDN'T TAKE MUCH MORE BEFORE IT WOULD FALL FORWARD. THEN ALL OF A SUDDEN THE CHAIN SNAPPED! THE GIANT ROCK STOOD STRAIGHT UP IN THE AIR! IT WOULDN'T HAVE TAKEN MORE THAN A LIGHT PUFF OF WIND TO BRING IT ON OVER; BUT THEN, THE BOTTOM OF THE ROCK STARTED TO SETTLE, AND THE TOP STARTED FALLING BACK TOWARD THE FACE OF THE BLUFF. AS THE GIANT BOULDER FELL BACKWARD, IT SLID DOWN, WITH THE BOTTOM OF THE ROCK SLIDING OUT TOWARD THE CREEK. THE ANGLE OF THE ROCK WAS MUCH FLATTER NOW, AND THERE WAS NO WAY WE'D EVER BE ABLE TO MOVE IT.

THERE WAS TOTAL SILENCE. THE ONE QUESTION IN EVERYONE'S MIND WAS, "WHAT DO WE DO NOW?" WE KNEW THAT DYNAMITE WAS OUT OF THE QUESTION. I HOLLERED TO RALPH, "BRING EVERYONE DOWN. WE'LL HAVE TO FIGURE OUT SOMETHING ELSE."

Nine

Rescue

I heard the rattle of harnesses and the sound of horses. More and more people were coming to help. As I turned to see who was coming, I saw Jack; Sally and Martha were with him. They were carrying baskets of food they'd prepared for the kids. I went to meet them so I could bring them up to date on what we'd been doing. As I approached the wagon, Sally sat down the baskets and ran to meet me. We embraced and tears began to flow. I could hear her saying, "Thank God you found them; thank God for Spike." Then she asked, "Are they all right?"

I said, "I'm not sure; I don't even know if they're among the ones who are alive." I told her everything that had happened and when I got through, she looked at me and said, "I know they're alive; I just know it!"

Jack said, "I brought the wagon most of the way. I had to leave it about a hundred yards back because the brush was too thick; I couldn't find a way through."

"I'm glad you thought of that," I said, "I know that when we get the kids out, some of them

WON'T BE ABLE TO WALK; THEY'LL BE TOO WEAK."

As we turned and started back toward the creek, I could hear Ralph hollering for me. When I answered him, he yelled, "Dave! I've found another entrance to the cave! It's a small crevasse that goes down through the ceiling! It's not big enough to get through, but with some sledgehammers and bars, we can soon make it large enough to get someone through!"

Everyone grabbed hammers and bars and headed upstream to find a way to the top of the bluff. I helped Sally and Martha with the food as we made our way to the top.

When we finally got to where Ralph was, several men were beating on the sandstone rock, trying to make the hole larger. Ralph said, "When I walked by the crevasse I could hear faint cries. I knelt down and put my ear near the hole and heard the children crying and begging for help."

I said, "Ralph, how much bigger does the hole have to be?"

He said, "I figure if we can make it another six inches wider and six inches longer, we can get someone through it."

By now, everyone had gathered around the hole, and we couldn't get close enough to see it. I could see that Bill Roberts was one of the men with a sledgehammer.

I hollered, "How's it coming, Bill?"

He yelled, "We'll have it big enough in another five minutes," and went back to swinging the hammer.

Everyone was very quiet and still; the only sounds that could be heard were the sounds of the hammers against the rock. I called out, "Did anyone bring a lantern?" Not a word was spoken, but three lanterns were raised into the air. The pounding sounds of the hammers continued to ring out, and I could feel my heart pounding in my chest; the rhythm of the beat was much faster than the hammers.

I had been able to make my way closer, and as Bill's hammer slammed against the rock, a big hole opened up as the weakened rock gave way. Everyone cheered and hollered.

The three men with lanterns were lowered by ropes to the floor of the cave, and everyone gathered near the hole, awaiting news. Then, word came up that they could see the kids, but there was a narrow passageway between them and the kids and they couldn't get through to them.

We could hear them calling to the kids, trying to get them to come through the small passageway, but the children were weak and unable to make it on their own.

One of the men, "Send Shorty Wilson down. He may be small enough to get through."

Shorty was a small man, about five feet tall; he probably weighed ninety pounds, soaking

WET. HE STEPPED FORWARD AND WITHOUT SAYING A WORD, TIED A ROPE AROUND HIS CHEST AND WAS LOWERED TO THE FLOOR OF THE CAVE. HE FOUND THAT HE COULD LAY ON THE FLOOR OF THE CAVE AND CRAWL THROUGH THE NARROW PASSAGEWAY, SO A ROPE WAS QUICKLY TIED TO HIS FEET TO HELP PULL HIM OUT IN CASE HE GOT STUCK. AFTER HE WAS SAFELY THROUGH THE PASSAGEWAY, HE SENT WORD UP THAT HE WAS ON THE OTHER SIDE, AND EVERYONE REJOICED BRIEFLY; THEN ONCE AGAIN, SILENCE FELL UPON THE CROWD AS THEY WAITED FOR MORE NEWS. THEN IT CAME -- SHORTY HAD FOUND THE KIDS AND EVERYONE WAS ALIVE!

THE CROWD COULD BE HEARD FOR MILES AND THEN THEY ALL BROKE DOWN IN TEARS; A NIGHTMARE WAS FINALLY COMING TO AN END.

SHORTY WILSON, THE MAN OF THE HOUR, WAS A VERY-HARD WORKING, WELL-RESPECTED MEMBER OF THE COMMUNITY. HIS SIZE WAS NEVER A FACTOR WITH HOW HE FIT IN. HE ALWAYS SAID, "A SMALL MAN CAN DO A BIG JOB." WELL, TODAY I LEARNED WHAT HE MEANT.

SHORTY STARTED WITH THE SMALLEST AND WEAKEST CHILDREN, AND ONE BY ONE, HE CARRIED THEM TO THE NARROW PASSAGEWAY AND TIED A ROPE AROUND THEIR CHESTS, THEN THE MEN ON THE OTHER SIDE PULLED THEM THROUGH. ONCE THROUGH THE PASSAGEWAY, THEY WERE PUT INTO A SWING AND HOISTED TO FREEDOM.

THE FIRST CHILD OUT WAS BECKY SWENSON. SHE WAS SIX YEARS OLD AND SO WEAK SHE COULDN'T STAND UP. HER EYES WERE SUNK WAY BACK IN HER HEAD, AND WHEN I LOOKED AT HER, A COLD FEELING

CAME OVER ME, LIKE DEATH WAS NEARBY. BECKY, NOW IN HER MOTHER'S ARMS SHOWED LITTLE RESPONSE. THEY BEGAN FEEDING HER SOME BROTH AND SHE COULD SWALLOW; THAT MEANT SHE HAD A GOOD CHANCE.

AS THE CHILDREN WERE LIFTED FROM THE CAVE, ONE BY ONE, THEY WERE FED AND CARED FOR. THE FOURTH CHILD OUT WAS TOM. A SMILE CAME TO HIS FACE WHEN HE SAW HIS MOTHER; AND THIS TIME, SALLY DIDN'T CRY. SHE WAS STRONG AND KNEW THAT WHAT TOM NEEDED NOW WAS CARE AND FOOD.

THE RESCUE WAS A SLOW PROCESS. IT TOOK MORE THAN AN HOUR TO GET ALL THE CHILDREN OUT OF THE CAVE. JAKE WAS THE LAST CHILD TO BE BROUGHT UP. HE WAS WEAK AND HUNGRY, BUT HE WAS GOING TO BE ALL RIGHT.

THE ONLY ONE LEFT TO BE BROUGHT UP WAS THE TEACHER. AS SHE WAS LIFTED FROM THE HOLE, SILENCE ONCE AGAIN CAME OVER THE CROWD, FOR THE TEACHER'S HUSBAND WAS ONE OF THE FARMERS WHO HAD DIED IN THE FIRE. SHE DIDN'T KNOW, AND WAS IN NO CONDITION NOW TO BE TOLD. AS SHE WAS LIFTED FROM THE SWING, SHE STARTED CALLING FOR HER HUSBAND, ZACK. ONE OF THE WOMEN INTERRUPTED HER BY GIVING HER A BOWL OF SOUP AND ENCOURAGING HER TO EAT. MRS. MILLER SEEMED TO FORGET ABOUT ZACK AS SHE BEGAN EATING.

SHORTY WAS THE FIRST MAN OUT OF THE HOLE, AND EVERYONE CHEERED AS HE CRAWLED OUT AND STOOD TO HIS FEET. SOMEHOW SHORTY STOOD MUCH TALLER IN MY EYES, AND I KNEW I'D NEVER AGAIN CALL HIM

Shorty. I didn't have anything against nicknames, but the name Shorty didn't do him justice.

Not many words were spoken for a long while, and then, as we began to see some response from the children, we started making plans to get them home.

Bonnie, the teacher, again asked, "Where's Zack?" Mr. Wilson knelt down, and taking her hand, told her that Zack had perished in the fire. She went limp, fainting in his arms. He gently picked her up and carried her to my wagon.

I told everyone to bring the children to my wagon, and I would take them to my house. They could bring their wagons there and pick them up.

We could get only half of the mothers and their children in our wagon. Bill Roberts said, "My wagon's only a short way from here. We can put the rest in it."

I said, "OK," so the rest of the children and their mothers followed Bill. Everyone else walked. As I untied the horses and got ready to leave, Sally turned to me and asked, "Where's Spike?" My God! I'd forgotten all about him. The last time I saw him he was lying on this side of the creek on the bank.

I said, "Jack, hold the horses." I ran back to look for Spike. When I got to the creek, there he was; he hadn't moved. I called to him and he raised his head and looked at me,

BUT WOULDN'T TRY TO GET UP. I WENT OVER TO HIM AND PICKED HIM UP AND CARRIED HIM TO THE WAGON.

I LAID HIM ON THE WAGON SEAT, AND JAKE CRAWLED UP BESIDE HIM. HE SAID, "I'LL HOLD HIM, DAD." I TOOK THE REINS AND LED THE HORSES TOWARD THE HOUSE.

IT TOOK A GOOD FIFTEEN MINUTES TO GET OUT OF THE WOODS AND ONTO THE ROAD; AND IT WASN'T LONG AFTER THAT TILL WE WERE PULLING UP IN FRONT OF THE HOUSE. IN A MATTER OF MINUTES, WAGONS AND BUCKBOARDS WERE PULLING UP TO TAKE THE CHILDREN HOME.

JACK AND MARTHA SPENT THE NIGHT AGAIN, AND EARLY THE NEXT MORNING BEFORE THEY LEFT, MARTHA FIXED A BIG BREAKFAST FOR THE BOYS WHILE JACK WENT WITH ME TO DO THE CHORES. THAT GAVE US A CHANCE TO TALK. WE HADN'T HIT IT OFF TOO WELL WHEN SALLY AND I FIRST GOT MARRIED, AND THINGS DIDN'T IMPROVE MUCH OVER THE YEARS.

WHEN WE GOT TO THE BARN, JACK SAID, "I'VE GOT SOMETHING ON MY MIND THAT I NEED TO TALK TO YOU ABOUT." WE SAT DOWN ON A COUPLE OF EMPTY KEGS, AND HE SAID, "DAVE, WHEN SALLY FIRST MARRIED YOU, I THOUGHT SHE WAS MAKING A BIG MISTAKE. I TOLERATED YOU BECAUSE OF HER. WELL, I'VE CHANGED MY FEELINGS ABOUT YOU. I THINK YOU'RE THE BEST SON-IN-LAW I HAVE; I COULD NEVER WISH FOR ONE BETTER." HE STOOD UP AND PUT OUT HIS HAND AND WE SHOOK.

I SAID, "JACK, I'VE GAINED A GREAT DEAL OF

107

RESPECT FOR YOU AS WELL." AND I KNEW THAT AFTER ALL THESE YEARS, JACK AND I HAD BECOME FRIENDS.

FOR THE NEXT SEVERAL DAYS, WE DID NOTHING BUT NURSE THE BOYS AND SPIKE BACK TO HEALTH. WE DIDN'T GO ANYWHERE OR SEE ANYONE. AFTER ABOUT A WEEK, THE BOYS WERE GETTING THEIR STRENGTH BACK AND THEIR FLESH WAS STARTING TO FILL OUT. THEY HAD LOST NEAR A THIRD OF THEIR WEIGHT WHILE THEY WERE ENTOMBED IN THE CAVE.

SPIKE WAS GETTING ALONG QUITE WELL, TOO, BUT HE WAS LIMPING REAL BAD ON HIS LEFT BACK LEG. I WASN'T SURE IT WOULD EVER BE NORMAL AGAIN, SINCE THE CUTS ON HIS HIP WERE DEEP INTO THE MUSCLE. HIS APPETITE WAS NORMAL AND HE WAS TRY- ING TO RUN SOME NOW.

ON WEDNESDAY OF THE FOLLOWING WEEK, THE PREACHER STOPPED BY TO GIVE A REPORT ON EVERYONE AND TO SEE HOW WE WERE DOING. IT SEEMED THAT ALL THE CHILDREN WERE GOING TO BE ALL RIGHT, BUT BONNIE WAS HAVING A TOUGH TIME OF IT. SHE AND ZACK HAD ONLY BEEN MARRIED FOR A SHORT TIME, AND SHE HAD NO FAMILY IN THE AREA. SHE HAD COME HERE FROM BATESVILLE TO TEACH SCHOOL, AND SHE WAS THINKING ABOUT GOING BACK THERE. IF SHE LEFT, WE'D BE WITHOUT A TEACHER; WE WERE ALREADY WITHOUT A SCHOOL.

THE PREACHER SAID, "WE'LL HAVE OUR CHURCH SERVICES AT THE SCHOOLYARD ON SUNDAY, AND THERE'S GOING TO BE A MEETING THERE AFTERWARDS."

AS HE GOT UP TO LEAVE, I SAID, "WE'LL BE

108

THERE SUNDAY FOR CHURCH AND WE'LL STAY FOR THE MEETING."

SUNDAY MORNING AFTER CHORING, SALLY AND THE BOYS, ALONG WITH SPIKE AND MYSELF, LOADED IN THE WAGON. WE HEADED FOR THE SCHOOLYARD.

SALLY HAD FRIED SOME CHICKEN AND MADE SOME POTATO SALAD THE NIGHT BEFORE. WE WERE GOING TO HAVE DINNER ON THE GROUND BETWEEN CHURCH SERVICES AND OUR COMMUNITY MEETING.

WHEN WE ARRIVED AT THE SCHOOLYARD, MANY OF THE CHILDREN WHO HAD BEEN TRAPPED IN THE CAVE WERE THERE PLAYING GAMES. BEFORE WE COULD GET IN PLACE AND STOP, THE BOYS AND SPIKE SLIPPED OFF THE BACK OF THE WAGON AND JOINED IN THE GAMES.

AS SOON AS THE KIDS SAW SPIKE AND ALL THE STITCHES ON HIS SIDE AND HIP, THEY STOPPED PLAYING AND LOOKED HIM OVER REAL GOOD. THEY TOOK TURNS PETTING HIM. THEY'D NEVER SEEN ANYTHING LIKE THAT BEFORE. THEY KNEW THAT SPIKE HAD NEARLY LOST HIS LIFE WHILE TRYING TO SAVE THEIRS.

I SAW JIMMY SMITH, THE OLDEST OF THE CHIL-DREN, RUBBING SPIKE, USING THE BACK OF HIS HAND. I REMEMBERED THE PREACHER TELLING US WHAT JIMMY HAD DONE FOR EVERYONE IN THE CAVE AND I WENT OVER TO TALK TO HIM. HE WAS KNELT DOWN BY SPIKE WHEN I GOT THERE, SO I KNELT DOWN BESIDE HIM; HIS HANDS WERE SOLID SCABS. HE WAS RESPONSIBLE FOR THE OTHER CHILDREN BEING ALIVE. IF IT HADN'T BEEN FOR HIM TAKING CHARGE AND SHOWING THEM HOW TO GET WATER, THEY MAY HAVE ALL DIED. I KNELT

109

THERE BESIDE HIM FOR A FEW MINUTES, AND NOT ABLE
TO THINK OF WHAT TO SAY, I GOT UP AND WENT BACK
TO WHERE SALLY WAS WAITING.

EVERYONE HAD BROUGHT CRATES, STOOLS, OR
KEGS TO USE FOR CHAIRS. THE PREACHER HAD PULLED
HIS BUCKBOARD INTO A POSITION TO WHERE HE COULD
USE IT AS A PULPIT. HE TOOK HIS PLACE ON IT AND
CALLED FOR SERVICES TO BEGIN.

AFTER CHURCH SERVICES WERE OVER, THE FOOD
WAS LAID OUT ON A LONG TABLE HASTILY MADE FROM
CRATES AND SLAB WOOD. I HAD ALWAYS ENJOYED THESE
COMMUNITY DINNERS BECAUSE THERE WAS ALWAYS LOTS OF
DIFFERENT FOODS, SALADS, CAKES AND PIES. NO ONE
WOULD GO HOME HUNGRY TODAY.

AFTER DINNER, SEVERAL SONGS WERE SUNG, AND
AROUND TWO O'CLOCK, THE PREACHER ONCE AGAIN TOOK
HIS PLACE ON THE BACK OF THE BUCKBOARD. HE MADE
EVERYONE AWARE OF OUR SITUATION AND OUR OPTIONS,
AND WHAT DECISIONS NEEDED TO BE MADE. HE SAID,
"THE FIRST ORDER OF BUSINESS IS TO ELECT A DIREC-
TOR -- SOMEONE WHO HAS GOOD LEADERSHIP QUALITIES
AND A STAKE IN THE COMMUNITY. WE NEED SOMEONE
WHO WILL MAKE SURE THE JOB GETS DONE. I SUGGEST
YOU TAKE A FEW MINUTES AND TALK IT OVER BEFORE WE
CONTINUE."

I WAS TRYING TO DECIDE WHO I'D LIKE TO
SUPPORT, WHEN GEORGE WILSON, THE ONE THEY CALLED
"SHORTY," CAME UP TO ME AND ASKED, "DAVE, WOULD
YOU CONSIDER FILLING THE POSITION?"

I HAD NEVER REALLY THOUGHT OF MYSELF DOING

110

SOMETHING LIKE THAT, BUT WHEN THREE MORE MEN REIN-
FORCED GEORGE'S REQUEST, I FELT THAT IF IT WAS
THE WISH OF THE MAJORITY, I'D GIVE IT MY BEST.

I SAID, "GEORGE, I'LL ACCEPT THE POSITION
IF YOU'LL BE MY ASSISTANT." HE AGREED.

WHEN THE MEETING WAS CALLED TO ORDER AGAIN,
NOMINATIONS FOR A DIRECTOR WERE ACCEPTED, AND I
WAS THE ONLY ONE NOMINATED.

AFTER BEING DULY ELECTED, I TOOK THE
PREACHER'S PLACE ON THE BUCKBOARD, FEELING ILL-AT-
EASE, SINCE I'D NEVER DONE ANYTHING LIKE THAT
BEFORE. I STOOD THERE, HOPING TO OVERCOME MY
NERVOUSNESS, AND WAS FINALLY ABLE TO SPEAK. ONCE
I GOT STARTED, I WAS NO LONGER NERVOUS. I AD-
DRESSED THE FIRST PROBLEM, SAYING, "OUR MAIN CON-
CERN RIGHT NOW IS THAT OF FINDING A PLACE TO HOLD
SCHOOL TILL A NEW SCHOOL CAN BE BUILT. DOES ANY-
ONE HAVE A SUGGESTION?"

JOE LARSON, WHO LIVED A SHORT WAY SOUTH OF
THE SCHOOL, AND WHOSE HOUSE AND BARN WERE BARELY
MISSED BY THE FIRE, SAID, "MY BARN CAN BE USED TO
HOLD SCHOOL IN AS LONG AS NEEDED."

AFTER SOME DISCUSSION, IT WAS AGREED THAT
JOE'S BARN WAS THE BEST LOCATION FOR THE TEMPORARY
SCHOOL.

I SAID, "THE NEXT PROBLEM WE NEED TO AD-
DRESS IS, WHAT ARE WE GOING TO DO ABOUT BONNIE
MILLER? SHE'S A GOOD TEACHER AND WE DON'T WANT
TO LOSE HER, BUT HER SITUATION IS GRIM. SHE LOST
HER HUSBAND IN THE FIRE; PLUS THEIR HOME, BARN

111

AND LIVESTOCK WERE DESTROYED. SHE HAS NO FAMILY
HERE AND IS STAYING WITH A NEIGHBOR, BUT THEY
DON'T REALLY HAVE ENOUGH ROOM TO KEEP HER LONG,
SO SHE NEEDS A PLACE TO LIVE. NOW, DOES ANYONE
HAVE A SOLUTION?"

THE CROWD GREW SILENT, TRYING TO THINK OF
A GOOD SOLUTION. THE SILENCE WAS FINALLY BROKEN
WHEN SOMEONE SUGGESTED WE BUILD LIVING QUARTERS IN
THE BACK OF THE SCHOOL. ANOTHER SUGGESTED WE
BUILD HER HOUSE BACK, SINCE SHE STILL HAD THE
LAND. THEN, TO MY SURPRISE, SALLY STOOD UP AND
SAID, "WHY DON'T WE GIVE MRS. MILLER SOME TIME TO
DECIDE WHAT SHE'D LIKE TO DO. IN THE MEANTIME,
DAVE AND I COULD CLOSE IN OUR BACK PORCH AND SHE
COULD STAY WITH US. I'VE BEEN WANTING TO CLOSE
THAT PORCH IN FOR A SPELL ANYWAY." THEN SALLY
TURNED TO BONNIE MILLER AND SAID, "WHAT DO YOU
SAY, BONNIE?"

BONNIE SAID, "I THINK THAT'S A GREAT IDEAL,
SALLY."

SALLY AND BONNIE WERE GOOD FRIENDS AND I
KNEW THIS WOULD BE A GOOD TEMPORARY ARRANGEMENT,
SO I SAID, "WELL, IT LOOKS LIKE THAT PROBLEM HAS
BEEN TAKEN CARE OF; NOW, THE NEXT THING WE NEED
TO ADDRESS, IS, WHEN AND WHERE DO WE BUILD THE
NEW SCHOOL?"

AFTER ONLY A COUPLE OF MINUTES, I GOT THE
IMPRESSION THAT THERE WAS NO QUESTION ABOUT IT;
THE SCHOOL WOULD BE BUILT BACK IN THE SAME PLACE,
USING THE SAME FOUNDATION. IT WOULDN'T TAKE LONG

112

TO CLEAN IT UP, AND EVERYONE WANTED TO GET START-
ED THE NEXT DAY.

I SAID, "WE'RE GOING TO TAKE UP A COLLEC-
TION TO BUY LUMBER FOR THE NEW SCHOOL, AND ALL OF
YOU NEED TO GIVE TILL IT HURTS. I'LL GO INTO
TOWN TOMORROW AND SEE WHAT KIND OF A DEAL I CAN
MAKE FOR THE LUMBER."

WELL, WE GOT ONE HUNDRED DOLLARS THAT DAY
IN DONATIONS AND PLEDGES. I FIGURED A NEW SCHOOL
WOULD COST ABOUT ONE HUNDRED AND EIGHTY DOLLARS TO
BUILD, BUT I FIGURED WE COULD USE THE SAME BELL,
SO THAT WOULD SAVE TWENTY DOLLARS.

I SAID, "IF THERE'S NO MORE BUSINESS, I
MOVE THAT WE ADJOURN THIS MEETING."

BEFORE ANYONE COULD SECOND THE MOTION, BOB
PHILLIPS SPOKE UP AND SAID, "THERE'S ONE MORE
MATTER THAT NEEDS TO BE DISCUSSED."

I ASKED, "WHAT'S THAT, BOB?"

HE SAID, "IF YOU'LL HELP ME UP THERE, I'LL
SHOW YOU." I TOOK BOB'S HAND AND HELPED HIM UP
ON THE BUCKBOARD. HE UNROLLED A PIECE OF PAPER
THAT READ:

THIS SCHOOL IS DEDICATED TO

SPIKE

"A HERO AND A LEGEND"

113

Bob said, "I'd like to make a plaque with this inscription on it and permanently affix it to the front of the new school."

Everyone cheered and clapped, signifying their approval. Bob added, "I'd also like to see this new school be named 'SPIKE'S SCHOOL.'" And again, everyone cheered.

I said, "I'll go along with the majority. Now, if there's nothing else, this meeting is adjourned."

On the way home, I said, "Sally, when do you plan on having Bonnie move in?"

She said, "I think we could have everything ready in about a week, don't you?"

I jokingly said, "That was a pretty sneaky way of getting that porch turned into a room."

She smiled and nudged me in the side with her elbow and said, "Yeah, it was, wasn't it?"

We both had a good laugh. She slid over close and put her arms around me, then kissed me and said, "I'm proud of you, Dave. I've also got a surprise for you."

I said, "Oh, yeah, what's that?"

She just grinned. All she said was, "Later." It was good to see her happy again.

Ten

The Return of the Bear

We were getting ready for bed and I said, "Sally, why don't you go to town with me tomorrow?" She agreed to go, so early the next morning after choring, we headed out with Spike and the boys. Spike was much better now. I said, "We'll have to remove his stitches soon."

She said, "We can do it today if we get home in time."

As we passed the school, there were already several people there cleaning up the mess. We didn't stop; we just waved as we went by. We had too much to do today to be lollygagging. I set the horses at a good pace, and they held it all the way to town. Sally and I were busy making plans, and the trip didn't seem to take long at all; as a matter of fact, it took just a little over an hour, according to my figuring.

We stopped in front of the grocery store. Sally and the boys got out and took the butter and eggs inside. Sally was going to do her shopping while I went to the bank and the lumberyard.

My first stop was the bank. The owner of the bank was Fred Cook. I'd known Fred all my

LIFE, BUT I'D NEVER DEALT WITH HIM PERSONALLY.
WHEN I WALKED IN, I ASKED TO SEE HIM, AND THE
TELLER SHOWED ME TO HIS OFFICE.

FRED LOOKED UP AND SAID, "COME IN, DAVE,
AND HAVE A SEAT," INDICATING A CHAIR IN FRONT OF
HIS DESK. I SAT DOWN AND HE ASKED, "TO WHAT DO
I OWE THIS UNEXPECTED PLEASURE?"

I SAID, "BONNIE MILLER'S HOME WAS DESTROYED
IN THE FIRE AND SHE DOESN'T HAVE A PLACE TO STAY.
IF SHE DOESN'T FIND A PLACE TO LIVE, WE'RE GOING
TO LOSE A GOOD TEACHER, BECAUSE SHE'LL HAVE TO
MOVE TO ANOTHER TOWN. WE'D LIKE TO CLOSE IN OUR
PORCH, MAKE IT PART OF THE HOUSE AND LET HER LIVE
WITH US FOR AWHILE. NOW, I FIGURE I NEED TO
BORROW TWENTY DOLLARS TO MAKE THAT PORCH INTO A
NICE ROOM FOR HER."

FRED SAID, "I HEARD ABOUT THE TRAGEDY OUT
YOUR WAY, DAVE; IT WAS JUST AWFUL." HE FILLED
OUT A FORM AND SAID AS HE HANDED IT TO ME,
"THERE'LL BE NO PROBLEM WITH YOUR LOAN. JUST
SIGN THIS AND GIVE IT TO THE TELLER. HE'LL GIVE
YOU THE TWENTY DOLLARS."

"JUST LIKE THAT?" I ASKED.

HE SAID, "JUST LIKE THAT."

I STOOD UP AND SAID, "WE TOOK UP A COLLEC-
TION TO BUILD A NEW SCHOOL, AND WE'RE EIGHTY DOL-
LARS SHORT OF BEING ABLE TO COMPLETE IT, BUT
WE'LL MANAGE SOMEHOW."

FRED SAID, "I'LL TELL YOU WHAT, YOU GET
WHATEVER YOU NEED TO BUILD THE SCHOOL, AND I'LL

STAND GOOD FOR THE BILL PERSONALLY. THE COMMUNITY CAN PAY IT AS SOON AS THEY'RE ABLE. AS A MATTER OF FACT, I'LL GO DOWN TO THE LUMBERYARD WITH YOU AND TAKE CARE OF IT RIGHT NOW."

ON THE WAY OUT OF THE BANK, I SIGNED THE NOTE AND GAVE IT TO THE TELLER. HE HANDED ME A TWENTY-DOLLAR BILL AND SAID, "WE APPRECIATE YOUR BUSINESS, SIR."

FRED AND I WALKED TO THE LUMBERYARD WHERE HE TOLD JOE, "GIVE DAVE THE SUPPLIES HE NEEDS TO BUILD THE NEW SCHOOL, AND I'LL STAND GOOD FOR THE BILL."

JOE SAID, "THAT'S FINE WITH ME. JUST TELL ME WHAT YOU NEED, DAVE, AND I'LL DELIVER IT FOR YOU."

FRED SHOOK MY HAND AND SAID, "I'LL SEE YOU LATER, DAVE. GOOD LUCK WITH YOUR PROJECT."

I FIGURED UP A MATERIAL LIST FOR THE PORCH AND ONE FOR THE SCHOOL AND GAVE THEM TO JOE.

I PAID FOR THE MATERIALS FOR THE PORCH AND GAVE HIM WHAT MONEY WE'D COLLECTED TOWARD THE SCHOOL. HE GAVE ME TWO RECEIPTS AND SAID, "I'LL START HAULING THE MATERIALS OUT TOMORROW."

I SAID, "I'D LIKE TO TAKE THE MATERIALS I NEED FOR THE PORCH WITH ME."

JOE NODDED AND SAID, "STOP BY ON YOUR WAY OUT OF TOWN, AND I'LL HAVE THEM READY FOR YOU."

AS I WALKED BACK TO THE GROCERY STORE, I TOOK MY MONEY OUT OF MY POCKET AND NOTICED THAT AFTER PAYING FOR THE MATERIALS FOR THE HOUSE, I

HAD TWO DOLLARS LEFT. WHEN I GOT TO THE STORE, I HANDED THE TWO DOLLARS TO SALLY AND SAID, "GET YOURSELF SOMETHING SPECIAL. WE'LL PICK YOU UP AFTER WE GET THE LUMBER AND MATERIALS LOADED." SHE SMILED AS SHE TOOK THE MONEY. I TURNED TO THE STORE OWNER AND SAID, "MIKE, I'LL BE BACK FOR THE SUPPLIES AFTER I LOAD SOME LUMBER."

WHEN I GOT IN THE WAGON, SPIKE AND THE BOYS SAW ME AND CAME RUNNING. WE WENT TO THE LUMBERYARD AND LOADED THE MATERIALS, THEN WENT BACK TO THE STORE AND LOADED THE SUPPLIES.

A FEW MINUTES LATER, SALLY CAME WALKING BRISKLY DOWN THE SIDEWALK WITH A BUNDLE UNDER HER ARM. SHE WAS SMILING AS SHE CLIMBED IN THE WAGON. I DIDN'T ASK HER WHAT SHE'D BOUGHT; I THOUGHT I'D LET HER TELL ME IN HER OWN TIME.

ABOUT HALF-WAY HOME, SHE TURNED TO ME AND SAID, "WELL!"

I SAID, "WELL, WHAT?"

"DON'T YOU WANT TO KNOW WHAT I BOUGHT?" SHE ASKED.

I SAID, "OK, WHAT'D YOU BUY?"

SHE OPENED THE BUNDLE AND I SAW A JEWELRY BOX INSIDE. IT HAD A MIRROR IN THE LID AND ONE SMALL DRAWER. IT WAS MADE OF RED CEDAR AND WAS POLISHED TO A LUSTROUS SHINE; IT WAS BEAUTIFUL.

SALLY SAID, "I'VE ALWAYS WANTED A JEWELRY BOX. SOMEDAY I'LL GIVE IT TO OUR DAUGHTER."

I LOOKED AT HER AND ASKED, "DO YOU KNOW WHAT YOU'RE SAYING?"

She said, "Why do you think I want that porch closed in?"

I said, "You tricked me, didn't you?" It looked like the boys would have, hopefully, a sister to play with. "And when's this supposed to happen?" I asked.

She said, "As best I can figure, in about nine months," and we both laughed. It was good to have her back to being herself.

After we got home, Sally couldn't wait to get started on the room. It was still early in the afternoon, and as she whipped up a quick dinner, I unloaded the wagon and put the team away.

After dinner, we went to work on the new room and worked till dark. That night, I looked the situation over and decided that with one more day's work, we'd have the room finished.

I said, "Sally, I'll have to work at the school for the next couple of days," and she agreed that I should. She started supper, and Jake and I went on to the barn. I had to light the lantern so I could see how to do the chores. Jake held the lantern. It felt good having him with me.

That night after we had finished supper, all Sally could talk about were the little details for finishing the new room. She knew exactly how she wanted it done.

The next morning, I chored early and headed for the school. I figured the lumber would start

119

ARRIVING ABOUT NOON. WHEN I GOT THERE, I WAS
REALLY SURPRISED TO SEE TWO WAGON LOADS OF LUMBER
SETTING IN THE SCHOOLYARD WAITING TO BE UNLOADED.

WE JUMPED IN AND UNLOADED THEM AS FAST AS
WE COULD. THE MEN WHO DROVE THEM OUT SAID, "JOE
HAD US LOAD THE WAGONS YESTERDAY, RIGHT AFTER YOU
PLACED THE ORDER. HE WANTED US HERE EARLY THIS
MORNING." IT WAS GOOD TO KNOW THAT PEOPLE CARED.

AFTER WE UNLOADED THE WAGONS, WE SORTED THE
LUMBER BY TYPE AND SIZE.

BY NOW, SEVERAL MEN WERE AT THE SCHOOL,
AND EVERYONE HAD BROUGHT SAWS, HAMMERS, YARD
STICKS AND SQUARES. THE CONSTRUCTION PROJECT
WOULD SOON BE UNDERWAY. WE HAD ONE MAN THERE WHO
HAD WORKED ON BUILDING HOUSES AND SCHOOLS, AND I
ASKED HIM TO TAKE OVER THE PROJECT. I COULD TELL
RIGHT OFF THAT I'D MADE A GOOD CHOICE BECAUSE HE
KNEW JUST WHAT TO DO.

AT DINNERTIME, MANY OF THE WOMEN SHOWED UP
WITH PICNIC LUNCHES. WE STOPPED JUST LONG ENOUGH
TO EAT AND THEN WENT BACK TO WORK. IT WAS ABOUT
FOUR O'CLOCK WHEN WE DECIDED TO CALL IT A DAY,
SINCE WE ALL HAD CHORES TO DO AT HOME.

AS SOON AS I GOT HOME, I SAID, "SALLY, I
NEED YOUR HELP. WE NEED TO TAKE THE STITCHES OUT
OF SPIKE'S SIDE."

"WHAT WILL WE NEED?" SHE ASKED.

I SAID, "GET A PAIR OF TWEEZERS AND
STERILIZE THEM." I GOT MY WHET STONE AND PUT A
RAZOR-SHARP EDGE ON MY KNIFE SO I COULD CUT THE

STITCHES CLEAN AND NOT HAVE TO DO SO MUCH PULLING. I DIDN'T WANT SPIKE TO SUFFER ANY MORE PAIN.

WE LAID HIM ON HIS SIDE, AND WHILE SALLY RUBBED HIS HEAD, I CUT THE STITCHES WITH MY KNIFE. THEN, ONE BY ONE, WE PULLED THEM OUT WITH THE TWEEZERS. IT TOOK ABOUT FORTY FIVE MINUTES TO GET THEM ALL OUT. SPIKE DID NOTHING MORE THAN FLINCH A COUPLE OF TIMES. AFTER THE STITCHES WERE OUT, HE CONTINUED TO LAY THERE, ENJOYING SALLY'S LOVING CARESS.

AT CHORE TIME, SALLY SAID, "I'LL HELP YOU WITH THE CHORES. I'VE GOT SUPPER READY TO PUT ON THE TABLE, AND I DON'T WANT TO JUST SIT AND WAIT FOR YOU TO GET THROUGH."

I FIGURED SOMETHING WAS UP; WHY ELSE WOULD SHE WANT TO GO WITH ME TO DO CHORES? SHE SAT AND WATCHED WHILE I DID THE MILKING AND DIDN'T SAY A WORD WHILE I GATHERED THE EGGS AND FED THE PIGS.

THE CHORES WERE DONE AND I WAS READY TO GO TO THE HOUSE, AND SALLY STILL HADN'T SAID A WORD. I SAT THE MILK BUCKET AND EGG BASKET ON THE GROUND, THEN TURNED TO HER AND SAID, "SALLY, THE CHORES ARE DONE, NOW TELL ME WHY YOU WANTED TO HELP."

SHE SHRUGGED HER SHOULDERS AND SAID, "I JUST WANTED TO SEE HOW LONG IT WOULD TAKE YOU TO GET CURIOUS." THEN SHE LAUGHED AND GRABBED THE EGG BASKET AND HEADED TOWARD THE HOUSE.

121

We ate supper and she put the boys to bed early. They were to start school the next day.

The next morning, I took the boys to the temporary school, then went on to help with the building of the new schoolhouse. There were several men already there.

I pitched in and began carrying boards and nails to whoever needed them. It seemed like every hour or so, we'd all get together and try to decide exactly how we wanted the school to look when it was finished. We had to decide on the number of windows, the size, and how high off the floor they needed to be. There was a lot of planning to be done. I hadn't realized just how much there was to do. I had figured we'd have this school built in just a few days, but I could see it was going to take a bit longer.

It was late morning when some one hollered, "Dave, it looks like you've got company coming."

I looked up and there came Sally waltzing down the road, carrying a basket. Her face was full of color and she had a glow about her; she was radiant and I knew she felt good. She came over to where I was working and sat down. I asked, "Where's Spike?"

She said, "He must have stayed with the boys; he didn't come back home this morning."

About that time, some of the other women arrived with more food, and we all stopped and ate dinner.

THE WEATHER TURNED OFF UNUSUALLY WARM, AND THERE WAS A LIGHT BREEZE FROM THE SOUTH. I STILL HAD SOME CORN IN THE FIELD, AND I KNEW I'D HAVE TO GET IT IN SOON. AND SINCE SALLY WANTED ME TO FINISH CLOSING IN THE ROOM, I TOLD EVERYONE THAT AFTERNOON WHEN WE QUIT THAT I'D HAVE TO BEG OFF FOR THE REST OF THE WEEK AND FINISH GETTING MY CROPS IN. THEY ASSURED ME THEY COULD HANDLE IT, SO I DIDN'T FEEL SO BAD ABOUT THEM HAVING TO GO AHEAD WITHOUT ME.

THE NEXT MORNING, SALLY HAD ME UP AND GOING AT FIRST LIGHT. SHE KNEW WHAT IT TOOK TO GET ME STARTED: A HOT CUP OF COFFEE AND A COUPLE OF EGGS. AFTER DOWNING THE COFFEE AND PUTTING THE EGGS AWAY, SHE SAID THAT I SHOULD HURRY THROUGH THE CHORES. WHEN I ASKED WHY THE HURRY, ALL I GOT WAS, "WE HAVE A LOT TO DO."

AFTER CHORING, SALLY INSISTED THAT WE WALK THE BOYS TO SCHOOL. WELL, THE BOYS KNEW THE WAY, BUT WE WOULD FEEL UNCOMFORTABLE LETTING THEM GO BY THEMSELVES JUST YET, SO WE FOLLOWED THE BOYS AND SPIKE, AS THEY HEADED OUT THROUGH THE WOODS, TAKING THE SHORTCUT TO SCHOOL.

IT WASN'T FAR THROUGH THE WOODS TO JOE LARSON'S PLACE. WHEN WE GOT TO HIS BARN, WHICH WAS SERVING AS THE TEMPORARY SCHOOL, BONNIE RAN OVER AND HUGGED SALLY AND ASKED, "HOW SOON CAN I MOVE IN?"

SALLY LOOKED AT ME AND SAID, "THIS WEEKEND, DON'T YOU THINK, DAVE?" SHE SHOOK HER FIST IN MY

123

FACE. I KNEW WHEN I'D BEEN HAD! I ALSO KNEW THAT ROOM WOULD BE FINISHED EVEN IF THE CORN WASN'T IN.

WHEN WE GOT BACK TO THE HOUSE, SALLY HEADED STRAIGHT FOR THE BARN. I HOLLERED, "HEY, WHERE ARE YOU GOING?"

SHE SAID, "I KNOW YOU WANT TO GET THAT CORN IN BEFORE YOU FINISH THE ROOM, SO I'M GOING TO HELP." THEN SHE SMILED AND ADDED, "I'VE PICKED A LITTLE CORN IN MY TIME."

WE HARNESSED THE TEAM AND LAID IN ON THE CORN. SALLY WAS A FINE WOMAN. I COULD HAVE LOOKED A LIFETIME AND NEVER FOUND ONE BETTER. SHE WAS STRONG AND OPINIONATED, BUT FAIR -- NOT JUST WITH ME, BUT WITH EVERYONE.

AS WE PULLED UP TO THE BARN WITH THE SEC-OND LOAD OF CORN, SALLY SAID, "I'LL FIX SOME SANDWICHES WHILE YOU START UNLOADING," AND HURRIED TO THE HOUSE.

I WAS THROWING THE LAST EARS OFF THE WAGON WHEN SHE WALKED INTO THE BARN AND ASKED IF I WAS READY TO EAT. WHILE I TIED THE FEED BAGS ON THE HORSES, SALLY SPREAD OUT A SHEET SHE WAS CARRYING, ON TO THE BACK OF THE WAGON, AND WE HAD A PICNIC LUNCH RIGHT THERE.

AFTER DINNER, WE LAY DOWN ON THE HAY AND RESTED FOR A SPELL. I WAS THINKING TO MYSELF, "THIS IS THE WAY LIFE WAS MEANT TO BE."

SALLY AND I GOT UP AND BRUSHED THE HAY OFF OUR CLOTHES AND HEADED BACK TO THE CORN FIELD,

AND BY SUNDOWN WE HAD ANOTHER TWO LOADS IN THE BARN. I SAID, "SALLY, IT LOOKS LIKE WE'LL HAVE ALL THE CORN IN BY NOON TOMORROW."

WHILE CHORING, I NOTICED SPIKE AND THE BOYS PLAYING OUTSIDE IN THE YARD. I COULD TELL HE WAS FEELING MUCH BETTER. HE WAS PLAYING AN OLD FAMILIAR GAME OF "CATCH ME IF YOU CAN" WITH THE BOYS. HE WAS RUNNING, CUTTING FAST AND JUMPING THE FENCE. HIS ENDURANCE WAS STILL LOW AND THEIR PLAY DIDN'T LAST LONG, BUT THINGS WERE GETTING BACK TO NORMAL. I WAS FEELING GOOD, TOO. I CAUGHT MYSELF WHISTLING WHILE I WAS FINISHING THE CHORES, AND I REALIZED THAT I WAS FEELING AS GOOD ABOUT THINGS AS I'D EVER FELT.

THE NEXT DAY AT NOON, AS I HAD PREDICTED, THE CORN WAS IN THE CRIB AND I COULD FINISH SALLY'S PROJECT. WE STARTED ON THE ROOM, AND BY NIGHTFALL, WE WERE READY TO ADD THE FINISHING TOUCHES.

THE NEXT MORNING, SALLY WANTED ME TO GO WITH HER TO WALK THE BOYS TO SCHOOL, SO I WENT ALONG. WHEN WE GOT TO LARSON'S BARN, SHE SAID, "BONNIE, EVERYTHING'S READY FOR YOU TO MOVE IN. WE'LL BE HERE WITH THE WAGON AS SOON AS SCHOOL IS OUT THIS AFTERNOON."

BONNIE SAID, "THAT'S GREAT! I'LL BE WAIT-ING."

SALLY AND I WORKED ON THE ROOM ALL DAY, TRYING TO MAKE IT AS COZY AS POSSIBLE, AND BY MID-AFTERNOON IT WAS READY. I HITCHED UP THE

125

WAGON AND SALLY AND I HEADED FOR THE LARSON'S TO HELP BONNIE LOAD UP HER THINGS AND MOVE THEM TO OUR HOUSE.

WHEN WE GOT TO THE SCHOOL, A GROUP OF MEN WERE STANDING AROUND A MAN ON A HORSE, TALKING. I PULLED THE WAGON UP NEXT TO THEM AND ASKED WHAT WAS GOING ON. THE MAN ON THE HORSE WAS BILL THOMPSON. HE SAID, "I WAS JUST TELLING THE MEN HERE THAT I SAW A BLACK BEAR COME OUT OF MY BARN. IT WAS THE BIGGEST BEAR I'VE EVER SEEN! IT WOULD PROBABLY STAND EIGHT FEET TALL!"

I HAD NEVER HEARD OF A BLACK BEAR GETTING THAT BIG. THERE WEREN'T MANY IN THIS PART OF THE COUNTRY, AND WHAT WERE HERE USUALLY STAYED AWAY FROM PEOPLE.

I SAID, "I REMEMBER A FEW YEARS BACK WHEN A KILLER BEAR HAD TO BE HUNTED DOWN AND DE-STROYED. I HOPE THIS ISN'T GOING TO BE ANOTHER ORDEAL LIKE THAT! SINCE WE DON'T HAVE A SCHOOL BELL TO RING TO SOUND AN ALARM, EVERYONE IN THE COMMUNITY WILL HAVE TO BE ALERTED BY MESSENGER." EVERYBODY NODDED IN AGREEMENT.

WE LAID OUT A PLAN ON HOW TO NOTIFY EVERY-ONE AND HOW TO GET REPORTS OF ANY SIGHTINGS TO BILL. PARENTS WERE TO BE TOLD TO TAKE THEIR KIDS TO AND FROM SCHOOL EVERY DAY. WE DIDN'T WANT TO TAKE ANY CHANCES BY LETTING THE KIDS GO HOME ALONE TODAY, SO I TOLD THEM THAT SALLY AND I WOULD STAY WITH THE KIDS TILL THEIR PARENTS CAME FOR THEM. THEY AGREED, AND THE MEN WENT IN ALL

DIRECTIONS TO SPREAD THE WORD ABOUT THE BLACK BEAR.

SALLY AND I WENT TO THE LARSON'S HOUSE AND ARRIVED JUST IN TIME TO CATCH THE KIDS BEFORE THEY STARTED HOME. WE TOLD THEM ABOUT THE BEAR AND THAT THEY WERE TO STAY HERE WITH US TILL SOMEONE CAME TO PICK THEM UP. MOST OF THE KIDS GOT SCARED, BUT A FEW OF THEM THOUGHT IT WAS EXCITING.

I STAYED CLOSE TO THE KIDS WHILE SALLY AND BONNIE STARTED LOADING THE WAGON WITH BONNIE'S THINGS. SHE DIDN'T HAVE MUCH, SINCE EVERYTHING SHE HAD OWNED WAS LOST IN THE FIRE. ALL THE NEIGHBORS HAD GIVEN HER AS MUCH AS THEY COULD. IT DIDN'T TAKE LONG FOR THEM TO LOAD EVERYTHING IN THE WAGON. THEY CAME OVER TO THE BARN WHERE THE KIDS AND I WERE PLAYING, AND SINCE I'D HAD ABOUT ENOUGH OF THEIR KIND OF PLAY, I BEGGED OFF AND LET THE KIDS PLAY BY THEMSELVES.

I WALKED OVER TO SALLY, AND SHE SAID, "DO YOU THINK THE BEAR THAT BILL SAW COULD BE THE SAME ONE THAT HURT SPIKE?"

I SAID, "THERE'S A GOOD CHANCE THAT IT WAS, SINCE THERE'S NOT MANY BEARS AROUND HERE."

"MAYBE WE'D BETTER KEEP SPIKE IN THE HOUSE," SHE SAID. "WE DON'T WANT HIM HURT AGAIN."

I SAID, "I AGREE. WE'D BETTER KEEP HIM CLOSE AT HAND. HE WAS LUCKY TO HAVE SURVIVED HIS FIRST ENCOUNTER WITH THE BEAR AND IT'S UNLIKELY

THAT HE'D BE ABLE TO SURVIVE ANOTHER."

WORD ABOUT THE BEAR SPREAD FAST, BECAUSE IT WAS ONLY A SHORT TIME BEFORE ALL THE KIDS HAD BEEN PICKED UP. WE LOADED IN THE WAGON AND HEADED HOME. TOM PUT HIS ARMS AROUND BONNIE AND KISSED HER ON THE CHEEK, THEN SAID, "I'M GLAD YOU'RE COMING TO LIVE WITH US, MRS. MILLER."

BONNIE PATTED HIS HAND AND SAID, "I'M GLAD TOO, TOM."

THE TRIP HOME WAS A LOT OF FUN. SALLY AND BONNIE WERE MAKING JOKES ABOUT EVERYTHING AND EVERYONE. I COULD TELL THAT IT WAS GOING TO BE GOOD FOR BOTH OF THEM, BEING NEAR EACH OTHER.

WHEN WE GOT HOME, I HELPED PUT BONNIE'S THINGS IN THE NEW ROOM. WHILE SHE AND SALLY ORGANIZED EVERYTHING, I DID THE CHORES. I FELT A BIT UNEASY; I DIDN'T KNOW IF THE BEAR WOULD SHOW UP AROUND HERE OR NOT. BILL'S PLACE WAS AL- MOST TWO MILES AWAY, BUT I KNEW THAT WASN'T FAR FOR A BEAR TO TRAVEL. I FOUND MYSELF VERY ALERT, AND AT THE SLIGHTEST SOUND, I'D LOOK AROUND TO SEE WHAT IT WAS. THE THOUGHTS OF A BEAR THAT BIG BEING ON THE ATTACK REALLY SCARED ME.

AFTER SUPPER, SALLY SAID, "DAVE, DO YOU THINK THE MILK YOU SAT OUT TO CLABBER, THE FIRST OF THE WEEK, IS READY TO MAKE COTTAGE CHEESE?"

I SAID, "I CHECKED IT WHILE I WAS CHORING AND IT WAS GOOD AND RIPE; JUST RIGHT!"

SHE SAID, "THAT'S GOOD, BECAUSE I WANT TO MAKE IT TOMORROW, AND I'LL NEED YOUR HELP."

"THE CREAM IS BUILDING UP, TOO, AND NEEDS TO BE CHURNED AS WELL," I SAID.

SHE SAID, "I GUESS WE'LL SPEND THE ENTIRE DAY GETTING CAUGHT UP."

THE NEXT MORNING AFTER CHORING, I TOOK THE CLABBER IN THE HOUSE AND CUT THROUGH IT WITH A KNIFE. IT CUT SMOOTH AND CLEAN AND THE CUT INSTANTLY FILLED IN WITH WHEY, WHICH MEANT THE CLABBER WAS JUST RIGHT FOR MAKING COTTAGE CHEESE.

FIRST, I CUT THE CLABBER INTO THIN STRIPS WHILE IT WAS STILL IN THE BUCKET. THEN, I CUT IT IN THE OTHER DIRECTION. THE TOP OF THE CLABBER NOW HAD SMALL SQUARES. THE NEXT STEP WAS TO DRAIN OFF ALL THE WHEY. AT THIS POINT, THE LARGE GLOB OF CLABBER HAD CHANGED TO ROUGH CURDS, AND AFTER I DRAINED THE WHEY OFF, SALLY AND BONNIE TOOK THE CURDS AND BROKE THEM BY HAND INTO SMALL CURDS. THEY TRIED TO MAKE THE CURDS AS UNIFORM IN SIZE AS POSSIBLE SO THEY WOULD TAKE THE SALT EVENLY. THEY ADDED THE SALT, THEN WORKED IT IN THOROUGHLY.

THE SALT STOPPED THE FERMENTING PROCESS OF THE MILK AND ALSO KILLED ANY BACTERIA THAT MIGHT HAVE CONTAMINATED THE CURDS.

SALLY PUT THE CURDS IN A PILLOWCASE AND HUNG IT ON THE CLOTHESLINE TO DRAIN. IT WOULD HAVE TO HANG FOR AT LEAST TWO HOURS. I SET A PAN UNDER IT TO CATCH THE WHEY SO I COULD FEED IT TO THE PIGS.

WHILE WE WAITED FOR THE CURDS TO DRAIN, I

129

BROUGHT IN THE SOURED CREAM. SALLY SKIMMED THE DRIED FILM OFF THE TOP AND STIRRED IN SOME SALT, PEPPER, MINCED ONION TOPS, AND TWO CLOVES OF CRUSHED GARLIC. THEN THEY SAMPLED THE SOURED CREAM. BONNIE SAID, "YOU KNOW WHAT THIS NEEDS? IT NEEDS A FEW CRUSHED WALNUTS."

SALLY SAID, "YOU'RE RIGHT."

I HEARD THEIR COMMENTS AND SAID, "SAY NO MORE." I WENT OUTSIDE AND CRACKED SOME BLACK WALNUTS. I TOOK THEM INSIDE, AND WE ALL SAT AROUND THE KITCHEN TABLE AND PICKED OUT THE WALNUT MEATS. SALLY MEASURED OUT TWO TABLESPOONFULS AND CRUSHED THEM WITH THE ROLLING PEN, THEN STIRRED THEM INTO THE SOURED CREAM. WE SAMPLED IT AND I SAID, "THIS IS GREAT!"

BONNIE TASTED IT AND SAID, "THIS WILL MAKE A GOOD DRESSING FOR THE COTTAGE CHEESE."

THE CURDS HAD BEEN HANGING FOR WELL OVER TWO HOURS WHEN I BROUGHT THEM INSIDE. SALLY DUMPED THEM INTO A LARGE PAN, AND USING THEIR HANDS, SHE AND BONNIE WORKED THE SOURED CREAM ALL THROUGH THE CURDS. THIS WAS THE FINAL STEP.

WE LET IT SIT FOR A COUPLE OF HOURS WHILE THE CURDS SOAKED UP THE SOURED CREAM, AND THEN THE COTTAGE CHEESE WAS READY TO EAT. IT WOULD KEEP FOR ABOUT TWO WEEKS, BUT THE WAY EVERYONE LOVED IT, I FIGURED IT'D BE GONE IN ABOUT A WEEK.

SALLY CLEANED THE CHURN WHILE I GATHERED UP THE REST OF THE CREAM. WE HAD ENOUGH CREAM TO MAKE TWENTY POUNDS OF BUTTER. IT WOULD TAKE TWO

CHURNINGS TO DO IT. I PUT THE OLD CREAM IN
FIRST. I KNEW THE BUTTERMILK FROM THE OLD CREAM
WOULD BE STRONG, SO I'D FEED IT TO THE PIGS. I
WOULD SAVE THE BUTTERMILK FROM THE FRESHER CREAM.

THE CHURN WAS MADE OF WOOD. IT WAS LARGE
AT THE BOTTOM, ABOUT A FOOT AND A HALF ACROSS,
AND WAS AROUND EIGHT INCHES ACROSS AT THE TOP.
THE TOP OF THE CHURN HAD A HOLE IN THE CENTER
FOR THE DASHER TO GO THROUGH. IT WAS ABOUT SIX
INCHES ACROSS IN AN X SHAPE WITH A HANDLE ABOUT
THREE FEET LONG.

ONCE EVERYTHING WAS IN PLACE, I BEGAN TO
CHURN BY MOVING THE DASHER UP AND DOWN. I WOULD
TAKE A SIX-TO EIGHT- INCH STROKE, AT THE RATE OF
ONE STROKE PER SECOND. WITH THE CREAM BEING
COLD, IT'D TAKE ABOUT AN HOUR AND A HALF FOR IT
TO BREAK OUT AND ANOTHER THIRTY MINUTES TO GATHER.
ALL IN ALL, IT'D TAKE ME ABOUT FOUR HOURS TO
CHURN BOTH BATCHES OF CREAM. AND AFTER THE CREAM
WAS CHURNED, IT WOULD TAKE SALLY ABOUT AN HOUR ON
EACH BATCH TO WORK IT, SALT IT AND BLOCK IT.
THE BEST BUTTER WAS MADE WHEN THE CREAM WAS WELL-
WATER TEMPERATURE OR ABOUT FIFTY-FIVE DEGREES.
THAT'S WHY WE KEPT THE CREAM LOWERED PART-WAY DOWN
IN THE WELL.

AFTER THE CHURNING WAS DONE AND I HAD A
CHANCE TO REST MY ARMS AND DRINK A CUP OF COFFEE,
IT WAS CHORE TIME. AS I GOT THE MILK BUCKET AND
STARTED FOR THE DOOR, SALLY HANDED ME A LARGE
GLASS OF BUTTERMILK AND SAID, "TRY THIS AND SEE

131

HOW IT WILL GO WITH SOME CORNBREAD, FRIED POTATOES AND BROWN BEANS."

SHE KNEW I LOVED BUTTERMILK. AS I DRANK IT DOWN, I SAID, "SALLY, THIS IS THE BEST BUTTERMILK I'VE EVER DRANK. THAT SECOND BATCH OF CREAM WAS AGED TO PERFECTION. I WON'T BE LONG CHORING IF YOU WON'T BE LONG MAKING THE CORNBREAD AND FRYING THE POTATOES."

I KNEW SHE HAD COOKED THE BEANS WHILE I WAS CHURNING, SO I HURRIED THROUGH THE CHORES. THAT NIGHT, WE HAD ABOUT AS GOOD A MEAL AS I'D EVER EATEN. THE BUTTERMILK AND COTTAGE CHEESE JUST TOPPED IT OFF.

Eleven

Dedication of the New School

It was Sunday morning so we got dressed and went to church. The services were being held in the open in the schoolyard. After the services were over, George Wilson walked up to me and asked, "Have you been squirrel hunting yet?"

I said, "I've been wanting to go, George, but I haven't made it to the woods."

"Well," he said, "if you'd like to go with me, I'll come by after dinner."

I knew George had a good hunting dog, and a mess of young squirrel would sure taste good, so I said, "Just stop by when you get ready to go and I'll be waiting." He walked away and we loaded in the wagon and headed home. No one had made mention of the bear. Maybe it was just an isolated incident and the bear had moved on. I sure hoped so; I'd hate to have to worry about a mean bear every minute of the day, especially one that big.

Shortly after dinner, George rode up with Dike, his hunting dog. I grabbed my rifle and walked out the door, and Jake was right behind me. He said, "I want to go too, Dad."

I turned around and said, "You'd better stay home, Jake, because of the bear. Maybe you can go next time."

He said, "Oh, shoot, Dad!" He stomped his foot and sat down on the porch.

Sally was standing in the door. I said, "We'll be back around chore time."

She said, "Get enough for supper."

George took the saddle and bridle off his horse and turned him loose in the corral. As we headed for the woods on foot, Spike came running from the house. I hollered to Jake, "Call Spike and keep him in the house. I don't want to take a chance of him meeting up with that bear."

Jake called Spike back to the house, and George and I walked toward the woods. Once we got far enough into the woods, George hollered, "Go, Dike! Go get 'em, boy!" Dike took off in a run, and it wasn't but a few minutes before he treed. He was a good hundred yards or so off to our right, and we stepped out at a pretty good clip, wanting to get there before the squirrel got away.

Dike continued barking real loud. George said, "When old Dike barks like that it means he can see the squirrel."

We could see Dike now. He had his front feet on a big white oak and was looking up into the tree, barking like crazy. As we approached the tree, we began scanning the limbs and branches

134

FOR THE SQUIRREL. GEORGE CIRCLED AROUND TO THE LEFT AND I WENT RIGHT. I CAUGHT A GLIMPSE OF GEORGE TAKING AIM AND I STOPPED AND WATCHED. JUST AS THE GUN WENT OFF, DIKE RAN TO HIM AND LOOKED UP. THE SQUIRREL WAS FALLING THROUGH THE LEAVES AND BRANCHES; GEORGE HAD GOTTEN IT!

AS THE SQUIRREL HIT THE GROUND, DIKE GRABBED IT IN HIS MOUTH AND BEGAN SHAKING HIS HEAD BACK AND FORTH. ONCE HE WAS SURE IT WAS DEAD, HE DROPPED IT AT GEORGE'S FEET. IT WAS A YOUNG GRAY AND WOULD BE GOOD AND TENDER. GEORGE PICKED IT UP AND WE HEADED OFF THROUGH THE WOODS. HE HOLLERED TO DIKE AGAIN, AND THE DOG TOOK OFF IN SEARCH OF A HOT TRAIL.

WE COULD STILL SEE HIM WHEN HE STARTED BARKING. WE RUSHED OVER TO FIND ANOTHER YOUNG GRAY HUGGING A LOW LIMB ON A SMALL SCALY-BARK HICKORY. AFTER BAGGING THE SECOND SQUIRREL, GEORGE SENT DIKE OUT AGAIN.

BY MID-AFTERNOON, WE HAD BAGGED EIGHT SQUIRRELS. SIX WERE GOOD FRYERS AND THE OTHER TWO WOULD HAVE TO BE BOILED. I SAID, "GEORGE, I THINK WE'VE GOT ENOUGH HERE TO HAVE A REAL FEAST." HE AGREED AND CALLED DIKE IN, AND WE HEADED FOR THE HOUSE.

SALLY SAW US COMING, AND SHE AND BONNIE RAN OUT TO SEE HOW MANY SQUIRRELS WE'D BAGGED. I SHOWED THEM HOW MANY WE HAD, AND SALLY SAID, "YOU AND GEORGE DRESS THE SQUIRRELS, AND BONNIE AND I WILL FIX A MEAL FIT FOR A KING."

George and I dressed the squirrels, then washed them and cut up the young ones. We left the old ones whole and put them in salt water. Sally could cook them tomorrow and make a mess of dumplings. We took them inside and set them on the cabinet. The girls had coffee waiting. We sat and talked for a spell, then George said, "Well, guess I'd better be getting on."

I said, "Nothing doing. You helped get them, now you have to help eat them."

Sally nodded and said, "That's right, George. You'd better stay for supper."

George agreed to stay. He didn't live far from us, so at chore time, we walked over to his place and did his chores, then came back and did mine. With that out of the way, we went back to the house.

Sally and Bonnie had supper almost ready, and they were setting the table. George and I sat down by the empty fireplace. I said, "There's a slight chill in the air, George. It could frost any day now; it's that time of year. Hog butchering time is only a month away. Are you going to butcher?"

He said, "Yeah, I figure on butchering at least one."

"Well," I said, "we could butcher together if you'd like."

He said, "I'd like that. Just let me know when you want to do it and I'll be ready."

136

Sally and Bonnie started setting the table and putting out the food. They had fried three squirrels, fixed mashed potatoes and gravy, and hominy. Sally set out a bowl of cottage cheese and a large pitcher of buttermilk. They had also made a big pan of biscuits, and there was honey and butter to go with them.

After supper, George said, "That sure was good, ladies. I can't remember ever having a meal that tasty."

I said, "I'll have to go along with you on that. Sally is a great cook!" We sat around the table and talked for a spell before George went home.

The next morning, we were concerned that the bear might still be around, so I took my gun and walked Bonnie and the boys to Larson's barn, then went on to the new school.

All the framework was now in place, and by noon we had the windows in and part of the siding on. None of the women showed up with lunches that day. They'd been told to stay home, because we weren't certain if the bear was still in the area or not. Everyone had brought their own lunch, and as we sat down to eat, the main topic of conversation was the bear.

Bill reported that no sightings had been made other than the one at his barn on Friday. Everyone was relieved, but agreed that we'd have to be cautious for awhile.

137

THAT AFTERNOON WE MANAGED TO GET MOST OF THE SIDING ON, SO ALL THAT WAS LEFT WAS SOME TRIM AROUND THE DOORS AND WINDOWS. WE DECIDED TO WAIT TILL THE NEXT DAY TO DO THE TRIM SINCE IT WAS TIME FOR SCHOOL TO LET OUT.

JOHN WEST, WHO WAS IN CHARGE OF CONSTRUCTION, SAID, "WE'LL NEED ALL THE HELP WE CAN GET TOMORROW, BECAUSE AFTER THE TRIMMING IS FINISHED, WE'LL HAVE TO HOIST THE BELL INTO THE BELL TOWER.

THE MEN WHO HAD KIDS IN SCHOOL HEADED FOR LARSON'S BARN. WHEN I GOT THERE, SPIKE WAS WAITING BY THE DOOR FOR THE BOYS. WE WAITED TILL BONNIE GOT THROUGH, THEN SPIKE AND I WALKED HER AND THE BOYS HOME.

SALLY WAS SITTING ON THE FRONT PORCH WAITING, AND WHEN SHE SAW US, SHE GOT UP AND WALKED OVER TO MEET US. SHE GRABBED MY HAND AND SAID, "I HAVE SOMETHING TO TELL YOU," AND LED ME TOWARD THE BARN. BONNIE AND THE BOYS WENT ON INTO THE HOUSE.

WHEN WE GOT TO THE BARN DOOR, SALLY STOPPED, THEN TURNED AND LOOKED ME IN THE EYE AND SAID, "DAVE, I THINK WE'RE GOING TO HAVE A BABY."

I HOLLERED, "WHOOPEE!" THEN I GRABBED HER AND SWUNG HER AROUND AND AROUND. BONNIE AND THE BOYS CAME RUNNING OUT AND WANTED TO KNOW WHAT WAS SO EXCITING.

TOM AND JAKE ASKED, "WHAT IS IT? WHAT'S GOING ON?"

BONNIE SAID, "I WANT TO KNOW, TOO."

138

"WE'RE GOING TO HAVE ANOTHER BABY!" SALLY TOLD THEM. TOM AND JAKE WHOOPED AND HOLLERED! THEY SAID, "MOM, WE WANT IT TO BE A GIRL!" BONNIE HUGGED SALLY AND TOLD HER HOW HAPPY SHE WAS FOR HER.

I WHISTLED AND HUMMED ALL THE TIME I WAS DOING THE CHORES. I SURE HOPED SALLY WAS GOING TO HAVE A GIRL THIS TIME. THE SUN WAS DOWN BY THE TIME I FINISHED THE CHORES, AND I NOTICED THAT THE CHILL IN THE AIR HAD A BITE TO IT. I FIGURED WE'D GET A HARD FROST TONIGHT. I TOOK THE MILK AND EGGS TO THE HOUSE, THEN WENT TO THE WOODPILE AND GOT SOME WOOD TO BUILD A FIRE IN THE FIREPLACE. I LAID IN A LITTLE EXTRA FOR THE NEXT MORNING. I KNEW A FIRE WOULD FEEL GOOD TONIGHT, AND IT WOULD FEEL EVEN BETTER IN THE MORNING.

JUST AS I'D THOUGHT, THE NEXT MORNING THERE WAS A HEAVY BLANKET OF FROST COVERING EVERYTHING. THIS FROST WOULD KILL THE LEAVES ON THE TREES AND DRIVE THE SAP INTO THE ROOTS. THE TREES WOULD LAY DORMANT FOR SEVERAL MONTHS.

THE BOYS ASKED, "WHY DID IT HAVE TO FROST SO EARLY?"

I SAID, "WELL, THE FIRST FROST IS JUST NA-TURES WAY OF WARNING US TO MAKE FINAL PREPARATIONS FOR WINTER."

THE NEXT SIXTY DAYS BEFORE HARSH WINTER SET IN WOULD BE UNPREDICTABLE. THE WEATHER USUALLY CHANGED FROM WARM TO COLD AND BACK TO WARM. I KNEW WHEN I LOOKED OUT AND SAW THE HEAVY FROST

THAT I'D SOON HAVE TO START CUTTING WOOD. I ALSO THOUGHT I'D TRY AND CLEAR ABOUT AN ACRE OF NEW GROUND TO PLANT TOMATOES IN NEXT YEAR, SINCE I FIGURED ON REPAYING FRED COOK, AT THE BANK, FROM WHAT I COULD MAKE OFF THE TOMATOES. AND WITH LUCK, I MIGHT HAVE ENOUGH LEFT OVER TO BUY A HORSE AND SADDLE. JAKE HAD BEEN AFTER ME TO GET ONE FOR QUITE A SPELL.

AS I WALKED BONNIE AND THE BOYS TO SCHOOL, THE MORNING SUN BEGAN WARMING THE FRIGID AIR AND THE FROST STARTED MELTING. IT WAS LIKE A LIGHT SPRINKLE AS WE WALKED THROUGH THE WOODS.

I LEFT THEM AT LARSON'S BARN AND WENT ON TO THE NEW SCHOOL. JOHN WEST WAS THE ONLY MAN THERE. HE WAS LAYING OUT A WORK PLAN FOR EVERYONE. WE SAT AND TALKED FOR A SPELL AND WAITED FOR THE OTHERS TO ARRIVE.

JOHN SAID, "WE'RE GOING TO HAVE TO HURRY AND GET THE SCHOOL FINISHED, BECAUSE EVERYONE'S GOING TO HAVE TO START CUTTING WOOD, AND HOG BUTCHERING TIME'S ONLY A MONTH AWAY. IT MAY TAKE US A FULL TWO WEEKS TO FINISH EVERYTHING AND GET THE SCHOOLYARD SMOOTHED."

AFTER THE OTHERS GOT THERE, WE HAD A MEETING AND EXPRESSED OUR CONCERN ABOUT WINTER COMING ON. EVERYONE AGREED TO SPEED UP THE WORK SO THE SCHOOL WOULD BE FINISHED AS SOON AS POSSIBLE.

WORK WAS IN FULL SWING, WHEN LATE THAT MORNING, SPIKE WALKED INTO THE SCHOOLYARD. EVERYONE SPOKE TO HIM AND ASKED HIM HOW HE WAS

DOING LIKE THEY EXPECTED HIM TO ANSWER. HE WALKED AROUND THE SCHOOL FOR A SPELL, THEN WENT INSIDE. THE MEN STOOD AND WAITED TO SEE WHAT SPIKE WAS DOING. AFTER A FEW MINUTES, HE WALKED OUT OF THE SCHOOL AND LEFT THE SCHOOLYARD, HEADING TOWARD THE LARSONS.

THE MEN ASKED, "WHAT WAS SPIKE DOING?"

I SAID, "I FIGURE HE HEARD THE NOISE AND JUST CAME TO SEE WHAT WAS GOING ON."

THE REST OF THAT WEEK, EVERYONE SHOWED UP EARLY. WE WORKED AS LATE AS WE COULD, BUT EVERY-ONE HAD CHORES TO DO, SO WE ALWAYS HAD TO GET HOME BEFORE DARK.

SATURDAY WAS THE DAY WHEN EVERYONE CAUGHT UP ON THEIR CHORES AT HOME, BUT BECAUSE OF THE NEED TO GET THE SCHOOL FINISHED, THEY ALL AGREED TO WORK ON THE SCHOOL SATURDAY, IN HOPES OF HAVING IT FINISHED BEFORE THE END OF THE FOLLOWING WEEK.

SINCE THERE WAS NO SCHOOL THAT SATURDAY, ALL THE WOMEN AND CHILDREN SHOWED UP AT THE SCHOOL. THE WOMEN COOKED DINNER OVER AN OPEN FIRE, AND THEN CLEANED UP THE MESS THE MEN HAD MADE AROUND THE SCHOOL. THEY PICKED UP SCRAPS OF WOOD AND A FEW NAILS THAT HAD BEEN DROPPED, AND THEY EVEN PICKED UP THE PILES OF SAWDUST.

THE CHILDREN PLAYED GAMES ALL DAY, FOR THE MOST PART. FROM TIME TO TIME, SOME OF THE OLDER ONES WOULD LEND A HELPING HAND WITH THE CLEAN UP BY PICKING UP THE SMALL PIECES OF WOOD. THOSE

SMALL PIECES WOULD MAKE GOOD KINDLING FOR STARTING A FIRE ON COLD MORNINGS.

SPIKE WAS THE MAIN ATTRACTION FOR THE CHILDREN. WITH HIS WOUNDS FULLY HEALED NOW, HE WAS PLAYING AS HARD AS EVER.

WHEN WE STOPPED FOR DINNER, A FEAST WAS LAID OUT ON SLAB WOOD-TABLES. THE PREACHER WAS THERE HELPING, AND AS HE ASKED THE BLESSING, SPIKE LAY ON THE GROUND AND PLACED HIS HEAD ON HIS FRONT FEET LIKE HE ALWAYS DID AT HOME. WHEN THE PREACHER SAID "AMEN," SPIKE REARED UP AND PUT HIS FRONT PAWS ON THE TABLE AND STARTED WHINING. EVERYONE LAUGHED.

BONNIE REACHED OVER AND PATTED SPIKE ON THE HEAD, THEN FIXED HIM A BOWL FILLED WITH CHOICE PIECES OF MEAT. SHE LEANED DOWN WITH THE BOWL, AND SPIKE TOOK IT IN HIS MOUTH AND CARRIED IT OVER TO A GIANT RED OAK WHERE THE KIDS USUALLY ATE. HE SAT THE BOWL DOWN AND BEGAN EATING, AND ALL THE KIDS GOT THEIR PLATES AND JOINED HIM.

AFTER SPIKE HAD LICKED HIS BOWL CLEAN, HE PICKED IT UP WITH HIS MOUTH AND TOOK IT OVER TO BONNIE. WE WERE SURPRISED THAT HE WOULD TAKE HIS BOWL TO HER. SHE SAW THE LOOKS ON OUR FACES AND SAID, "I ALWAYS BRING A LITTLE EXTRA LUNCH TO SCHOOL TO SHARE WITH SPIKE. THAT'S WHY HE TOOK THE BOWL FROM ME AND BROUGHT IT BACK TO ME TO REFILL."

BONNIE TOOK THE BOWL FROM SPIKE AND REFILLED IT, THEN, WITH HIM BY HER SIDE, SHE TOOK

IT OVER WHERE THE CHILDREN WERE EATING AND SET IT DOWN.

AFTER DINNER, EVERYONE SAT AND TALKED FOR A SPELL. THE SUBJECT OF THE BEAR CAME UP, AND NO ONE HAD SEEN IT. WE WERE SATISFIED NOW THAT THE BEAR HAD LEFT THE AREA.

WE ALL WENT BACK TO WORK, AND BY QUITTING TIME, WE WERE READY TO START THE PAINTING ON THE OUTSIDE. WE HELD A SHORT MEETING BEFORE LEAVING FOR THE DAY AND DECIDED THAT SUNDAY WEEK, AFTER CHURCH, WE WOULD HAVE A COMMUNITY DINNER AND DED-ICATION CEREMONY FOR THE NEW SCHOOL. WE EN-COURAGED EVERYONE TO NOTIFY AS MANY PEOPLE AS THEY COULD BECAUSE WE WANTED IT TO BE A SPECIAL SERVICE AND A LOT OF FUN.

THE NEXT MORNING, WE WENT TO CHURCH AND HELD THE SERVICES OUTSIDE THE NEW SCHOOL. THERE WAS A BREEZE OUT OF THE NORTH AND IT WAS QUITE COOL. NO ONE WASTED ANY TIME ABOUT HEADING HOME AFTER THE SERVICES WERE OVER.

SALLY AND BONNIE WERE FIXING DINNER WHEN GEORGE KNOCKED ON THE DOOR. I INVITED HIM IN, AND SALLY POURED US A CUP OF COFFEE. WE SAT AND TALKED WHILE THE GIRLS FINISHED PREPARING DINNER.

WHEN DINNER WAS READY, GEORGE GOT UP TO LEAVE. SALLY INSISTED THAT HE STAY AND EAT. AFTER A TIME, HE FINALLY AGREED AND WE ALL SAT DOWN TO EAT. GEORGE SAT ACROSS THE TABLE FROM BONNIE AND I COULD TELL FROM THE LOOKS THAT WERE PASSING BACK AND FORTH BETWEEN THEM THAT SALLY AND

I WOULD BE SEEING A LOT OF GEORGE WHILE BONNIE WAS LIVING WITH US.

AFTER DINNER, GEORGE AND I WENT FOR A WALK THROUGH THE WOODS AND TALKED ABOUT THE NEW SCHOOL, THE WEATHER, THE HOG BUTCHERING THAT WAS GOING TO HAVE TO BE DONE SOON, AND JUST WHATEVER ELSE CAME TO OUR MINDS.

WE HAD MADE A BIG CIRCLE AND WERE ON OUR WAY BACK TO THE HOUSE. I KEPT THINKING ABOUT THE LOOKS THAT HAD GONE BACK AND FORTH ACROSS THE TABLE BETWEEN GEORGE AND BONNIE. I SAID, "GEORGE, WHAT DO YOU THINK ABOUT BONNIE?"

HE SAID, "I THINK SHE'S ABOUT AS BEAUTIFUL A WOMAN AS I'VE EVER SEEN. I'D LIKE TO COURT HER WHEN THE TIME'S RIGHT."

I SAID, "I THINK BONNIE IS A FINE WOMAN. A MAN COULD DO A SIGHT WORSE."

WE TALKED ABOUT THE TWO OF THEM FOR QUITE A SPELL, AND I SUDDENLY REALIZED THAT BONNIE WAS THE REASON FOR GEORGE'S VISIT. I SMILED AS WE MADE OUR WAY BACK TO THE HOUSE.

THE GIRLS WERE SITTING AT THE TABLE DRINKING COFFEE. WE JOINED THEM AND TALKED FOR A SPELL. IT WAS GETTING ON TOWARD CHORE TIME WHEN GEORGE HEADED HOME.

WHEN I WENT TO THE BARN TO DO THE CHORES, SALLY WENT WITH ME AND I TOLD HER ABOUT THE CON-VERSATION I'D HAD WITH GEORGE. SHE SAID, "BONNIE AND I HAD A SIMILAR CONVERSATION. SHE LIKES GEORGE, BUT DOESN'T FEEL COMFORTABLE WITH SEEING

144

ANYONE JUST YET; IT'S TOO SOON." THEN SHE SMILED, ADDING, "WHEN THE TIME IS RIGHT, WE NEED TO HELP THEM GET TOGETHER."

"HOW DO WE KNOW WHEN THE TIME IS RIGHT?" I ASKED.

SHE SAID, "WE'LL KNOW," AND LET IT GO AT THAT. I FIGURE THERE ARE SOME THINGS THAT MEN WEREN'T MEANT TO UNDERSTAND.

MONDAY MORNING, WITH THE FEAR OF THE BEAR GONE, BONNIE TOOK THE BOYS AND HEADED DOWN THE PATH THROUGH THE WOODS TO LARSON'S BARN. I TOOK THE ROAD AND WENT TO WORK ON THE NEW SCHOOL.

ALL THAT WAS LEFT WAS THE DESK AND THE PAINTING. THE DESK WAS BEING PUT TOGETHER OUTSIDE WHILE THE INSIDE OF THE SCHOOL WAS BEING PAINTED. WE PAINTED EVERY DAY, AND BY THURSDAY EVENING, WE WERE READY TO SET THE FURNITURE IN.

FRIDAY MORNING, WE SET THE DESK INSIDE, THEN HUNG THE BLACKBOARD AND SET THE POT-BELLIED STOVE IN PLACE. WE HAD SOME EXTRA TIME SO WE CUT AND RICKED A COUPLE OF RICKS OF WOOD.

JUST BEFORE WE HEADED HOME, WE ACKNOWLEDGED TO OURSELVES AND TO EACH OTHER THAT WE HAD DONE A FINE JOB. THE NEW SCHOOL WAS A CREDIT TO EVERYONE THERE.

SUNDAY MORNING, FOR THE FIRST TIME IN TWO MONTHS, THE SCHOOL BELL STARTED RINGING. IT COULD BE HEARD FOR MILES AROUND. IT WAS A GOOD SOUND AND IT WAS A PROUD DAY.

AS WE MADE OUR WAY TO CHURCH, THE BELL

145

CONTINUED TO RING, AND WHEN WE PULLED INTO THE SCHOOLYARD, WE SAW A LARGER TURNOUT THAN WE'D EVER SEEN BEFORE.

AFTER CHURCH SERVICES WERE OVER, WE HAD A COMMUNITY DINNER FIT FOR A KING. THE CHILDREN AND SPIKE DID MORE PLAYING THAN EATING.

AROUND THREE O'CLOCK, THE PREACHER CALLED FOR EVERYONE'S ATTENTION. IT WAS TIME FOR THE DEDICATION CEREMONY TO BEGIN.

BILL PHILLIPS HURRIED TO HIS WAGON AND GOT SOMETHING FROM UNDER THE SEAT. WE WATCHED AS HE UNWRAPPED IT. WHEN HE CAME BACK, HE HAD A BIG SMILE ON HIS FACE. HE WENT UP TO THE FRONT OF THE GROUP WHERE THE PREACHER WAS AND HANDED HIM A LARGE PLAQUE MADE OF SOLID WALNUT. ON THE PLAQUE WAS AN INSCRIPTION, BURNED INTO THE WOOD. IT READ:

THIS SCHOOL

IS DEDICATED TO

SPIKE

"A HERO AND A LEGEND"

So THE SCHOOL WAS DEDICATED TO SPIKE, IN
HIS HONOR. AS BILL NAILED THE PLAQUE TO THE WALL
IN THE FOYER NEXT TO THE FRONT DOOR OF THE
SCHOOL, EVERYONE CHEERED. IT WAS NOW OFFICIAL.

THE NEW SCHOOL WAS FINISHED, AND BONNIE WAS
LOOKING FORWARD TO HOLDING CLASSES IN IT THE NEXT
DAY.

TWELVE

SPIKE TAKES A MATE

It was now early December and the first winter storm had set in. There was a strong wind out of the north and the clouds looked heavy with snow. George and I had planned on butchering today, but we were going to have to put it off till after the storm passed.

Bonnie asked if I'd go to the school and ring the bell to signify "no school" today. She was the one who had the say about whether there'd be school on bad days.

When I got to the school, I rang the bell. Three rings, a pause, and then three more rings. I repeated it several times so everyone would hear.

I went back home and stood in front of the fireplace to get warm. My hands and feet were almost frozen. The wind was strong and the temperature was near zero.

After I had warmed up a little, I was laying in some kindling for the cook stove, and on my second trip out, I could see small snowflakes being carried by the wind. They seemed to be moving parallel to the ground.

149

As I was making my way back to the house, I saw George leaning into the wind, coming my way. I stopped on the porch and waited for him. When he finally made it to the porch, I opened the door and we went inside. I said, "A cup of that coffee would sure taste good, Sally."

She said, "Coming right up," and got up to get some cups out of the cabinet.

Bonnie said, "Hi, George. It's good to see you again."

"It's good to see you, Bonnie." he replied.

Bonnie, standing near the fireplace, said, "Come over here and warm yourself."

George walked over to the fireplace and stuck his hands out toward the fire. After a few seconds, he rubbed them together, then held them out again. He looked at Bonnie and said, "It sure is cold out there."

She smiled and said, "I know it is. That's why I called off school today."

While Sally was pouring the coffee, we glanced over at Bonnie and George. They were staring at each other and neither was saying a word. Sally nudged me, then smiled and winked as she whispered, "The time is right." Then she raised her voice and said, "Coffee's ready."

We sat at the table and talked for a long spell. Sally and Bonnie fixed dinner, and George stayed and ate with us.

After we'd finished eating and had talked for awhile, he got up and put on his coat and said, "Guess I'd better head home and tend to things."

I said, "George, as soon as the weather breaks we can butcher."

He asked, "Would it make butchering go faster if I brought my pig over here? We could butcher all of them at one time."

I nodded and said, "That's a good idea. Let's do that."

After George left, there was nothing to do but try and stay warm till chore time. The boys and Spike were beginning to get on Sally's nerves. They hadn't been outside all day, and they were starting to roughhouse quite a lot. Every time she'd get after them they'd calm down for a few minutes and then they were right back at it. As I watched them, I could tell that Spike was the big culprit; he would lie still for a few minutes, then start tugging at their clothes, wanting to play, and it wasn't long till they were all over each other.

The next morning, it was just as cold as it had been the day before, and the wind was even worse; but by mid-afternoon, the wind had laid, and the temperature seemed to rise a little.

There was a good three inches of snow on the ground, and Sally sent the boys and Spike outside to play. I got their sled out of the

BARN, AND THEY HAD FUN THE REST OF THE AFTERNOON.

I WAS STILL CHORING WHEN THE SUN STARTED DOWN AND THE TEMPERATURE BEGAN DROPPING A LITTLE. SALLY HAD CALLED THE BOYS INSIDE, BUT SPIKE HAD REMAINED OUTSIDE. AS I STARTED FOR THE HOUSE, I CAUGHT A GLIMPSE OF HIM HEADING INTO THE WOODS. I FIGURED HE WAS GOING TO CHECK OUT WHATEVER HE'D BEEN SMELLING OR SENSING ALL DAY, AND HE'D BE BACK IN A LITTLE WHILE. I KNEW IT WASN'T A BEAR BECAUSE IT WAS MUCH TOO COLD; THEY'D BE IN HIBERNATION TILL LATE FEBRUARY.

EVERY SO OFTEN I'D GO OUT ON THE PORCH AND CALL SPIKE, BUT HE DIDN'T COME BACK AT ALL THAT NIGHT. THE NEXT MORNING WE TRIED TO FIND HIM, BUT HE WAS NOWHERE AROUND.

BY MID-AFTERNOON, IT HAD WARMED UP A BIT. THE TEMPERATURE WAS ABOVE FREEZING. THERE WAS STILL NO SIGN OF SPIKE. I SAID, "SALLY, I'M GOING TO GEORGE'S AND HELP HIM MOVE HIS PIG OVER HERE SO WE CAN BUTCHER TOMORROW." I WALKED OUT THE DOOR, PUTTING MY COAT ON AS I WENT.

GEORGE AND I DIDN'T HAVE ANY TROUBLE MOVING HIS PIG IN WITH MINE. HE WAS EASY TO HANDLE BE- CAUSE IT WAS SO COLD. AFTER GETTING THE PIG IN THE PEN, WE WENT INTO THE WOODS AND GATHERED UP SEVERAL DEAD LIMBS SO WE COULD BUILD A FIRE AROUND THE BARREL FOR SCALDING THE HOGS.

GEORGE STAYED AROUND TILL CHORE TIME BEFORE HEADING HOME. I KNEW HE WAS BEGINNING TO LIKE BEING AROUND MY PLACE.

When it got dark and there was still no sign of Spike, we started getting worried. I wondered if he, like his mother, couldn't resist the call of the wild. Spike was now six, and his urges and instinct to be with his own kind would be stronger than it had ever been before. I figured time would tell, and there was nothing we could do but wait.

The next morning, Spike still hadn't come home. By the time I got through choring, George was there to help with the butchering. The weather was much better today, and since it was Saturday, there was no school.

While Sally and Bonnie were fixing breakfast, George and I hung the block and tackle in the big oak tree near the pig pen. We sat the barrel on some rocks and filled it half full of water. We built a big fire around the barrel, using the dead wood we had gathered the day before. While we waited for the water to get hot, we went in and ate breakfast. While we were eating, we mapped out our strategy for the day.

We thought we'd scald and scrape all three hogs before we started butchering. Then, while we were butchering, the girls could start rendering lard and making chitlings and cracklings. I belted down the last of my coffee and said, "If everyone's ready, let's get started." We took our coats off the pegs by the door and put them on as we went out.

AFTER KILLING AND BLEEDING THE HOGS, WE CUT
THE TENDONS AWAY FROM THE BONE, NEAR THE HOCK,
AND HOOKED THEM TO A SINGLETREE, SO THEY COULD BE
HOISTED UP AND LOWERED INTO THE BARREL OF SCALDING
WATER. WE COULD SCALD A HOG TWICE AND SCRAPE IT
CLEAN IN FIFTEEN MINUTES.

AFTER THE HOGS WERE SCRAPED, THEY WERE HUNG
BY THE BACK LEGS, JUST HIGH ENOUGH THAT THEIR
HEADS CLEARED THE GROUND BY TWO FEET. GEORGE AND
I CUT THE HOGS OPEN AND PUT ALL THE INSIDES IN
A WASHTUB. THE LIVER WAS TAKEN OUT FIRST AND
WOULD HAVE TO BE COOKED TODAY. IT WAS THE ONE
THING THAT WOULDN'T KEEP LONG. THERE WAS NO
QUESTION ABOUT WHAT WE WERE HAVING FOR DINNER AND
SUPPER. THE KIDNEYS AND HEART WERE PLACED IN A
SEPARATE PAN SO THEY COULD BE GROUND INTO SAUSAGE.

SALLY AND BONNIE STRIPPED THE FAT OFF THE
INTESTINES WHILE GEORGE AND I CLEANED THE FAT FROM
THE INSIDE OF THE HOGS. WE PUT THE FAT IN THE
WASH KETTLE WHICH WAS HOT FROM THE FIRE WE'D
STARTED EARLIER. IT WOULD YIELD TO THE HEAT AND
WHAT WAS LEFT WOULD BE LARD AND CHITLINGS. WE
WOULD STORE THE LARD IN FIVEGALLON CANS AND USE
IT FOR COOKING, MAKING SOAP, AND OILING HARNESS
AND BOOTS. WE'D USE THE CHITLINGS TO FLAVOR
BEANS AND CORNBREAD.

AFTER ALL THE INTESTINES WERE STRIPPED OF
THEIR FAT, WE CUT THEM INTO PIECES ABOUT TWO FEET
LONG, THEN EMPTIED, INVERTED AND WASHED THEM. WE
ALSO EMPTIED AND WASHED THE STOMACH. IT WOULD BE

USED FOR STORING HOGSHEAD CHEESE AND SAUSAGE WHEN IT WAS MADE.

WHEN WE BUTCHERED, WE DIDN'T THROW AWAY ANYTHING BUT THE LUNGS AND THE EYES. WE USED EVERYTHING ELSE.

AFTER THE FAT WAS REMOVED FROM THE THREE CARCASSES AND PUT IN THE KETTLE TO RENDER, WE CUT OFF THE HAMS, SHOULDERS, BACON SLABS AND JAWS. THESE WE RUBBED DOWN WITH A SPECIAL MIXTURE WE HAD MADE. IT WAS A BLEND OF SALT, HONEY, BROWN SUGAR, WILD MUSTARD SEED, GARLIC AND PEPPER. THIS MIXTURE WOULD PRESERVE THE MEAT AND KEEP IT FROM SPOILING.

IT WOULD TAKE ABOUT THREE WEEKS FOR THE MEAT TO CURE, THEN, AFTER CURING, WE WOULD COLD SMOKE SOME OF IT, AND THE REST WE WOULD SLOW COOK AND HOT SMOKE. THIS PROCESS MADE HAM SO GOOD YOU'D WALK A MILE JUST TO SMELL IT.

AFTER THE MEAT TO BE CURED WAS SALTED DOWN AND HUNG IN THE SMOKEHOUSE, ALL THAT WAS LEFT WAS MAKING THE SAUSAGE AND RENDERING THE SKIN TO MAKE CRACKLINGS AND MORE LARD.

WE REMOVED THE SKIN OFF THE MEAT WE HAD SAVED FOR SAUSAGE, AND CUT THE SKIN INTO PIECES AN INCH WIDE AND TWO INCHES LONG, THEN PLACED IT IN THE KETTLE AND RENDERED IT. IT WAS THEN CALLED CRACKLINGS. WE SALTED IT AND WOULD USE IT AS NEEDED.

WE PUT THE HOGS' FEET AND EARS IN A CROCK OF VINEGAR AND SALT FOR PICKLING. WE GROUND THE

REST OF THE MEAT INTO SAUSAGE, SAVING A SMALL AMOUNT FOR THE HOGSHEAD CHEESE.

AFTER THE SAUSAGE WAS GROUND, WE TOOK IT INSIDE. WE WERE WORKING IN THE SPICES WHEN WE HEARD A NOISE AT THE DOOR. WHEN SALLY OPENED IT, THERE STOOD SPIKE. SHE LET HIM IN AND FED HIM SOME OF THE LIVER. HE ATE LIKE HE WAS STARVED, SO SHE GAVE HIM SOME MORE. HE FINALLY ATE HIS FILL AND THEN WANTED OUTSIDE. WHEN SALLY OPENED THE DOOR, SPIKE RAN OUT AND HEADED TOWARD THE HILLS. I RAN AFTER HIM, CALLING HIS NAME, BUT HE KEPT GOING. WHEN HE GOT TO THE EDGE OF THE CLEARING, A GRAY WOLF STEPPED OUT TO MEET HIM. I KNEW SHE'D BEEN WAITING THERE FOR HIM TO COME BACK TO HER.

SALLY AND I HAD ALWAYS SAID WE WOULDN'T TRY TO KEEP SPIKE FROM DOING WHATEVER HE WANTED, AND IF HE WANTED TO BE WITH HIS OWN KIND, IT WOULD BE WITH OUR BLESSING. WE WERE SADDENED BY HIS DECISION TO LEAVE, BUT WE WENT BACK TO MAKING THE SAUSAGE.

AFTER THE SEASONING WAS MIXED IN GOOD, WE STUFFED IT INTO THE CLEANED INTESTINES. WE PUT A TWIST IN THE LONG LINK ABOUT EVERY EIGHT INCHES AND TIED IT OFF WITH A STRING. THIS WOULD MAKE A GOOD CUT OF SAUSAGE WITHOUT EXPOSING THE CUT TO THE AIR. ONCE ALL THE SAUSAGE WAS PACKED AND HUNG IN THE SMOKEHOUSE, WE CLEANED UP THE MESS WE'D MADE. ALL WE HAD TO THROW AWAY WERE A FEW BONES THAT HAD BEEN PICKED CLEAN.

It had been a week since Spike had left home, and we sure missed him. The weather had warmed up and school was back in session, and Christmas was only a week away. This was the last day of school till after the holidays were over. Sally and I were working on Christmas presents for the boys. Sally was making them shirts to match, and I was making them a new wagon. I usually made all their toys, and Sally made most of their clothes. All I lacked having the wagon finished was painting it, but I'd have to finish it in the barn to keep the boys from finding it.

That afternoon, when the boys came in from school, guess who was leading the pack! You got it -- Spike! It was like he had never been gone. He had a family in the wild. That wasn't the first time we had seen him with her. We were afraid that one day he'd leave and never come back.

With Spike back home, I knew the boys would be playing in the barn, so I said, "Sally, I think I'll take the wagon over to George's house to finish it." She walked with me to the barn and said, "Have George come over for dinner tomorrow."

"Now what are you cooking up?" I asked.

All she'd tell me was, "You get George over here and you'll see."

I took the wagon to George's house, and he

HELPED ME PUT A COAT OF PAINT ON IT. WHEN I GOT READY TO LEAVE, I SAID, "SALLY'S PLANNING ON YOU COMING FOR DINNER TOMORROW."

WITH A PUZZLED LOOK ON HIS FACE, HE SAID, "WELL, OK. I'LL BE THERE."

ON THE WAY HOME, I DECIDED THAT GEORGE WASN'T THE ONLY ONE WHO WAS PUZZLED; I WAS PUZZLED, TOO.

THE NEXT MORNING, AROUND ELEVEN O'CLOCK, BONNIE PUT ON HER COAT. WHEN SALLY ASKED HER WHERE SHE WAS GOING, SHE SAID, "OH, I LEFT SOME PAPERS AT SCHOOL THAT I NEED. I'LL BE BACK SOON."

AROUND NOON, GEORGE SHOWED UP. SALLY SAID, "BONNIE SHOULD HAVE BEEN BACK BEFORE NOW. I'M CONCERNED ABOUT HER. GEORGE, WOULD YOU MIND CHECKING ON HER?" AND, OF COURSE, GEORGE SAID HE'D BE GLAD TO AND LEFT TO FIND BONNIE.

AS SOON AS HE WALKED OUT THE DOOR, SALLY PUT DINNER ON THE TABLE AND SAID, "WE CAN GO AHEAD AND EAT."

"WHAT ABOUT BONNIE AND GEORGE?" I ASKED.

SHE SAID, "THEY CAN EAT WHEN THEY GET BACK."

"THEY'LL BE BACK IN FIFTEEN OR TWENTY MINUTES," I SAID, THINKING SALLY WAS A LITTLE IMPATIENT TODAY.

"OH, I THINK IT'LL BE MORE LIKE A COUPLE OF HOURS," SHE SAID, SO I DIDN'T SAY ANYTHING ELSE. I SAT DOWN AND ATE DINNER, AND SURE NUF,

ALONG ABOUT TWO THIRTY, GEORGE AND BONNIE WALKED IN.

TOM RAN TO BONNIE AND SAID, "I WAS LOOKING OUT THE WINDOW AND SAW YOU TWO HOLDING HANDS COMING DOWN THE ROAD." GEORGE'S FACE TURNED BEET RED!

SALLY SCOLDED TOM AND SENT THE BOYS TO THE BARN TO PLAY, THEN APOLOGIZED FOR NOT WAITING DINNER. SHE SAID, "THE BOYS WERE HUNGRY AND DIDN'T WANT TO WAIT, SO WE WENT AHEAD AND ATE."

BONNIE SAID, "THAT'S OK. I HAD MORE TO DO AT SCHOOL THAN I THOUGHT."

"YOU TWO SIT DOWN AND I'LL GET YOUR DINNER," SALLY SAID, ADDING, "I KEPT IT HOT FOR YOU."

WELL I WAS FINALLY GETTING THE PICTURE. IT LOOKED LIKE SALLY AND BONNIE HAD SUCCESSFULLY WORKED THEIR LITTLE PLAN.

THE CHRISTMAS PROGRAM WAS TO BE HELD AT THE SCHOOL ON CHRISTMAS EVE AND BONNIE WAS IN CHARGE OF IT. THE PROGRAM WOULD BE SHORT, THEN EVERYONE WOULD GET A SACK OF CANDY AND NUTS. BONNIE WAS RESPONSIBLE FOR GETTING THE SACKS READY. SHE LOOKED UP AT GEORGE AND ASKED, WITH ONE OF THOSE FUNNY GIRL SMILES, "GEORGE, WOULD YOU HELP ME WITH THESE SACKS? WE NEED TO FILL THEM WITH ALL THESE DIFFERENT CANDIES AND NUTS."

GEORGE GRINNED AND SAID, "SURE, IT'LL BE FUN. THAT IS, IF I CAN SAMPLE THE CANDY AND NUTS."

159

Sally said, "Bonnie, I want to keep it a secret from Tom and Jake, so when you get ready to fill the sacks, why don't you take everything over to George's house and get the sacks ready over there so the boys won't see them."

George said, "I'd be more than happy to let you use my house to fill the sacks, Bonnie. After all, I'm going to help."

Bonnie smiled and said, "That's nice of you, George. Could you bring your wagon over early Monday morning? We'll haul everything to your house, and that way, we can take our time getting the sacks ready."

"I'll be here bright and early," George promised.

By the time Bonnie and George finished dinner, it was near supper time, and I still had chores to do, so I went on to the barn and took care of things in short order.

When I got through the chores, George was gone. The boys and Spike were playing in the bedroom, and Sally and Bonnie were sitting in front of the fireplace plotting and planning. At least, that's what I thought they were doing; for every few words, they'd laugh and giggle like a couple of teenage girls. It sure was good to see Sally and Bonnie so happy.

Well, Monday morning, George drove up in his wagon to get Bonnie and the Christmas candy and nuts. I figured the entire job of filling

THE INDIVIDUAL SACKS SHOULD TAKE ABOUT THIRTY MINUTES, BUT BONNIE DIDN'T GET HOME TILL JUST BEFORE DARK.

THE NEXT MORNING, BONNIE WALKED OVER TO GEORGE'S HOUSE AND SPENT THE DAY AGAIN, SUPPOSEDLY WORKING ON SOMETHING TO DO WITH CHRISTMAS. THEY DID FINISH PAINTING THE BOYS' WAGON.

ON CHRISTMAS EVE, BONNIE WALKED OVER TO GEORGE'S BECAUSE HE WAS GOING TO TAKE HER AND THE SACKS OF CANDY TO THE SCHOOL. SALLY AND I TOOK THE BOYS AND SPIKE WITH US.

WHEN WE GOT TO THE SCHOOL, JOHN WEST WAS DRESSED UP LIKE SANTA CLAUS, AND HE WAS GREETING ALL THE CHILDREN AS THEY ARRIVED.

THE PROGRAM WAS EXCEPTIONALLY GOOD, AND AFTER IT WAS OVER, SANTA HANDED OUT A SACK OF CANDY AND NUTS TO EVERY PERSON THERE. EVERYONE SEEMED TO HAVE A GOOD TIME.

GEORGE BROUGHT THE BOYS' WAGON BY THAT NIGHT AND SET IT OFF AT THE BARN, AND LATER THAT NIGHT, AFTER THEY WENT TO SLEEP, I BROUGHT IT INTO THE HOUSE AND SET IT BY THE TREE.

THE BOYS GOT UP BRIGHT AND EARLY CHRISTMAS MORNING. THEY FOUND THEIR WAGON AND NEW SHIRTS UNDER THE TREE FIRST THING. THEY SPENT THE ENTIRE DAY OUTSIDE PLAYING WITH THE WAGON AND SPIKE.

Thirteen

One Life for Another

GEORGE AND BONNIE WERE SEEING A LOT OF EACH OTHER NOW. HE WALKED HER TO AND FROM SCHOOL EVERY DAY. EVERY TIME I SAW ONE, I SAW THE OTHER.

IT HAD BEEN A REAL COLD WINTER, AND IT SEEMED TO ME THAT I HAD SPENT ALL MY TIME EITHER CUTTING WOOD OR PUTTING IT ON THE FIRE.

IT WAS NOW THE MIDDLE OF FEBRUARY, AND THE WEATHER WAS STARTING TO BREAK. IT WAS STILL COLD, BUT NOT NEARLY AS COLD AS IT HAD BEEN, AND THE COLD SNAPS WERE LESS FREQUENT. IT WAS THE TIME OF YEAR WHEN WINTER AND SPRING FIGHT FOR DOMINANCE.

IN LATE FEBRUARY, WE HAD A WARM SPELL AND THE GROUND WAS JUST RIGHT FOR TURNING. I HITCHED THE HORSES TO THE PLOW AND STARTED PLOWING, GETTING READY TO PLANT SPRING OATS. ABOUT MID-AFTERNOON, THE SCHOOL BELL BEGAN RINGING. I KNEW IT MEANT SOMETHING WAS WRONG, SO I UNHARNESSED THE TEAM AND HEADED FOR THE SCHOOL.

WHEN I GOT THERE, A CROWD HAD ALREADY GATHERED. I ASKED WHAT WAS WRONG, AND JIM WHITT SAID EXCITEDLY, "I SAW A BIG BLACK BEAR COMING

163

OUT OF MY BARN AROUND NOON. WHEN I CHECKED, I
FOUND TWO OF MY YOUNG CALVES THAT WERE ONLY TWO
WEEKS OLD DEAD AND PARTIALLY EATEN!

I SAID, "IT LOOKS LIKE THAT BEAR DIDN'T
LEAVE OUR AREA LAST FALL AFTER ALL; IT'S BEEN IN
HIBERNATION. NOW THERE'S REAL CAUSE FOR CONCERN.
WE'D BETTER SPREAD THE WORD!"

SO, WORD ABOUT THE BEAR WAS QUICKLY SPREAD
THROUGHOUT THE COMMUNITY, AND EVERYONE WAS ON
WATCH. I CARRIED MY RIFLE EVERYWHERE I WENT,
EVEN WHILE I WAS DOING MY CHORES.

SALLY WAS CLOSE TO SEVEN MONTHS PREGNANT.
SHE WAS WORRIED ABOUT THE BOYS WALKING TO SCHOOL
WITH THE BEAR AROUND. BONNIE SAID, "DON'T WORRY,
SALLY, I'M GOING TO CANCEL SCHOOL UNTIL THREATS OF
THE BEAR ARE GONE."

SO, THE NEXT MORNING WHEN CHURCH SERVICES
WERE OVER, BONNIE ANNOUNCED, "SCHOOL WILL BE
DISCONTINUED UNTIL THE BEAR IS DEAD, OR UNTIL THE
MEN FEEL IT'S SAFE TO RESUME SCHOOL."

AFTER SERVICES, WHILE EVERYONE WAS STANDING
AROUND TALKING, DICK JONES RODE UP TO THE SCHOOL.
HE LIVED ABOUT TWO MILES AWAY. HIS HORSE WAS ALL
LATHERED, AND WE KNEW HE'D BEEN RIDING HARD. HE
SAID EXCITEDLY, "THE BEAR ATTACKED AND KILLED ONE
OF MY COWS -- A FULL-GROWN COW!"

NOW EVERYONE WAS IN A PANIC BECAUSE THE
BEAR HAD KILLED AGAIN. IT HAD BEEN IN HIBERNA-
TION ALL WINTER AND WAS HUNGRY. IT WAS TOO EARLY
FOR BERRIES AND ALL THE NATURAL FOODS THAT BEARS

EAT, SO IT HAD KILLED FOR FOOD, AND WE FIGURED THAT ONCE IT HAD TASTED BLOOD, IT COULDN'T STOP.

WE ORGANIZED HUNTING PARTIES WITH EACH GROUP HAVING FIVE MEN. THE MEN WERE TO TAKE THEIR FAMILIES HOME, GET THEIR GUNS AND MEET BACK AT THE SCHOOL AS SOON AS POSSIBLE.

I TOOK SALLY AND THE BOYS AND BONNIE HOME AND GOT MY GUN, THEN HEADED BACK TO THE SCHOOL. I TOOK SPIKE ALONG, HOPING HE'D TRACK THE BEAR, BUT HE'D NEVER BEEN USED FOR HUNTING ANIMALS AND I DIDN'T KNOW IF HE WOULD TRACK THE BEAR OR NOT.

THE MEN WENT TO THE LAST PLACE THE BEAR HAD KILLED TO START THE SEARCH. I TRIED BUT COULDN'T GET SPIKE TO PICK UP THE TRAIL. MY GROUP HEADED DOWN THE CREEK, WHILE THE OTHER GROUPS HEADED IN DIFFERENT DIRECTIONS, IN HOPES OF SIGHTING THE BEAR.

THE MEN MET BACK AT THE SCHOOL JUST BEFORE SUNDOWN. THERE HAD BEEN NO SIGHTINGS OF THE BEAR. WE AGREED TO MEET AGAIN THE NEXT MORNING, AND EVERYONE HEADED HOME, WANTING TO GET THEIR CHORES DONE BEFORE DARK. I WASTED NO TIME IN DOING MINE. I DIDN'T WANT TO BE OUTSIDE AFTER DARK. I KEPT SPIKE WITH ME WHILE I DID MY CHORES, FIGURING HE COULD SMELL THE BEAR COMING BEFORE I COULD HEAR IT, AND I HOPED THAT IF HE DID SMELL IT, HE'D SOMEHOW LET ME KNOW. WHEN I FINISHED THE CHORES, I PUT ALL THE ANIMALS IN THE BARN AND FASTENED THE DOOR.

WE WERE ALL RESTLESS THAT NIGHT. I

COULDN'T SLEEP FOR WORRYING ABOUT THE BEAR AND WHERE IT MIGHT SHOW UP NEXT. AS SOON AS IT WAS GOOD AND LIGHT, I TOOK SPIKE WITH ME AND GOT THE CHORES OUT OF THE WAY.

WHEN I GOT READY TO GO TO THE SCHOOL, I SAID, "SALLY, KEEP SPIKE WITH YOU TODAY; THAT WAY, IF THE BEAR COMES AROUND, HE'LL SCARE IT AWAY. AND BE SURE TO KEEP EVERYONE IN THE HOUSE." I SLIPPED OUT THE DOOR AND SHE LOCKED IT BEHIND ME.

I GOT TO THE SCHOOL AT NINE O'CLOCK. WE DIVIDED INTO FOUR GROUPS AND HEADED OUT IN FOUR DIFFERENT DIRECTIONS. MY GROUP WAS GOING BY JOE LARSON'S PLACE TO SEE ABOUT HIM BECAUSE HE'D SAID HE WOULD BE JOINING US THIS MORNING AND HE DIDN'T SHOW UP. IF SOMEONE SAW SOMETHING, HE WAS TO FIRE SEVERAL SHOTS AND WAIT FOR THE OTHERS.

WHEN WE GOT TO THE LARSON'S, THE BARN DOOR WAS OPEN, AND WE FIGURED THEY WERE STILL CHORING. WHEN WE WALKED INTO THE BARN, A SICK FEELING CAME OVER US, FOR THERE IN THE MIDDLE OF THE BARN WERE THE BODIES OF JOE AND SUE. THEY HAD BEEN RIPPED AND TORN INTO SHREDS. ALL THE ANIMALS IN THE BARN WERE DEAD AND MANY HAD BEEN PARTIALLY EATEN.

THE BEAR HAD NOW HAD A TASTE OF HUMAN BLOOD, AND WE KNEW IT WAS JUST A MATTER OF TIME TILL IT WOULD KILL AGAIN. NO ONE WOULD BE SAFE TILL THE BEAR WAS HUNTED DOWN AND DESTROYED.

WE FIRED SEVERAL SHOTS INTO THE AIR, AND WHILE WAITING FOR THE OTHERS TO ARRIVE, WE LOOKED FOR SIGNS TO TRY AND DETERMINE WHICH WAY THE BEAR

HAD GONE. FROM THE SPOTS OF BLOOD WE WERE ABLE TO FIND, THE BEAR SEEMED TO BE HEADING FOR THE HILLS, JUST TO THE SOUTH.

I KNEW THIS HAD TO HAVE HAPPENED THIS MORNING WHILE JOE AND SUE WERE DOING THEIR CHORES, AND IT WAS ONLY A QUARTER OF A MILE TO MY HOUSE. EVEN THOUGH THE SIGNS SHOWED THE BEAR HAD HEADED TOWARD THE HILLS, I WAS AFRAID HE MIGHT HAVE DOUBLED BACK AND ENDED UP AT MY PLACE. AS THE OTHER SEARCH TEAMS ARRIVED, TENSION AND FEAR BEGAN TO GROW. THEY WERE HORRIFIED BY WHAT THEY SAW AND KNEW THE BEAR HAD TO BE FOUND, AND HAD TO FOUND NOW.

WE REORGANIZED OUR SEARCH PLAN AND DECIDED TO SPREAD OUT IN PAIRS, TO COVER AS MUCH AREA AS POSSIBLE, BUT ALWAYS KEEPING IN SIGHT OF EACH OTH-ER.

I WENT OVER TO GEORGE AND SAID, "LET'S PAIR UP TOGETHER. I'D LIKE TO GO BY AND CHECK ON SALLY AND THE BOYS AND BONNIE." HE NODDED AND WE MADE A QUICK TRIP TO MY PLACE.

I WAS RELIEVED WHEN WE FOUND EVERYONE SAFE AND SOUND. WE ASKED SALLY AND BONNIE TO JOIN US ON THE PORCH SO THE BOYS COULDN'T HEAR WHAT WE WERE SAYING, THEN WE TOLD THEM WHAT HAD HAPPENED TO JOE AND SUE. THEY BOTH GOT A LITTLE HYS-TERICAL, AND IT TOOK SOME TIME TO CALM AND COMFORT THEM.

WHEN WE GOT READY TO LEAVE, I SAID, "MAKE SURE THE BOYS DON'T GO OUTSIDE. I DON'T WANT

167

THEM LEAVING THE HOUSE TILL I GET HOME THIS EVE-
NING. WE'LL BE SEARCHING IN THE AREA TOWARD THE
HILLS, AND THERE'S LITTLE CHANCE OF THE BEAR GET-
TING AROUND US WITHOUT BEING SEEN, BUT I WANT YOU
TO BE CAREFUL."

GEORGE AND I REJOINED THE OTHERS, AND WE
SPREAD OUT AND STARTED SEARCHING AGAIN. WE HAD
TRAVELED ABOUT TWO MILES AND THERE HAD BEEN NO
SIGN OF THE BEAR, SO WE DECIDED TO MOVE OVER AND
SEARCH BACK IN THE OTHER DIRECTION. WE FEARED
THE BEAR MAY HAVE DOUBLED BACK. THIS PASS WOULD
TAKE US BY MY PLACE, AND IT WOULD GIVE ME ANOTHER
CHANCE TO CHECK ON SALLY AND THE BOYS. WITH
SALLY BEING SEVEN MONTHS PREGNANT, SHE DIDN'T NEED
ALL THE STRESS RELATED TO THIS BEAR.

WE MOVED OVER AND LINED UP AND WERE NOW
HEADING DUE NORTH, LOOKING CLOSELY FOR ANY SIGN.
IT WAS HARD TO BELIEVE THAT A BEAR AS BIG AS THE
ONE WE WERE LOOKING FOR COULD JUST DISAPPEAR
WITHOUT LEAVING A LOT OF SIGNS AROUND.

BACK AT THE HOUSE, SALLY AND BONNIE WERE
COOKING DINNER AND DIDN'T HEAR TOM GO OUT. SALLY
PUT DINNER ON THE TABLE AND CALLED OUT, "JAKE,
YOU AND TOM COME EAT YOUR DINNER." JAKE AND
SPIKE CAME OUT OF THE BEDROOM, AND SALLY ASKED,
"WHERE'S TOM? TELL HIM TO COME EAT."

"HE CAME IN HERE A LITTLE BIT AGO," JAKE
REPLIED.

SALLY WENT INTO THE BEDROOM, THINKING TOM
WAS HIDING. AFTER A QUICK SEARCH, SHE REALIZED

THAT HE WASN'T IN THE HOUSE AND SCREAMED, "OH, MY GOD!" AND RACED TO THE DOOR. SHE RAN OUT ON THE PORCH AND HOLLERED FOR TOM, BUT THERE WAS NO ANSWER. SHE CALLED AGAIN AND AGAIN WHILE HER EYES WERE SCANNING THE AREA. SHE CAUGHT A GLIMPSE OF SOMETHING NEAR THE CREEK, JUST TO THE NORTH OF THE HOUSE. IT WAS TOM; HE WAS PLAYING AT THE CREEK AND WAS TOO FAR AWAY TO HEAR HER. JUST AS SHE STEPPED OFF THE PORCH, THE BEAR WALKED OUT OF THE WOODS, NOT THIRTY FEET FROM TOM! IT REARED UP AND HEADED FOR HIM, AND SALLY, SCREAMING, RACED TOWARD THEM!

TOM HEARD SOMETHING AND TURNED TO SEE THE BEAR ONLY A FEW FEET AWAY, COMING STRAIGHT FOR HIM! HE STARTED RUNNING, BUT STUMBLED AND FELL.

SALLY WAS SCREAMING AT THE TOP OF HER LUNGS AND RUNNING AS FAST AS SHE COULD! TOM WAS SCURRYING AROUND, TRYING TO GET TO HIS FEET AND GET AWAY FROM THE BEAR! JUST AS SALLY GOT TO HIM, SHE REACHED DOWN TO HELP HIM UP, AND AT THAT VERY INSTANT, SPIKE LUNGED AT THE BEAR FROM ABOUT TEN FEET AWAY AND GRABBED IT BY THE THROAT!

THE IMPACT OF SPIKE'S UNEXPECTED ATTACK WAS ENOUGH TO KNOCK THE BEAR OFF BALANCE. HIS MIGHTY PAW BARELY GRAZED SALLY, KNOCKING HER DOWN.

THE BEAR RIPPED SPIKE LOOSE FROM ITS THROAT, THEN THREW HIM ABOUT TWENTY FEET ACROSS THE CLEARING. BY THIS TIME, SALLY AND TOM HAD GOTTEN TO THEIR FEET AND WERE RUNNING TOWARD THE HOUSE. THE BEAR, STANDING ABOUT EIGHT FEET TALL,

LOOKING LIKE A FEROCIOUS GIANT, TOOK OFF AFTER THEM!

AGAIN SPIKE LEAPED AND GRABBED THE BEAR BY THE THROAT! IT WAS ROARING AND SLAPPING AT SPIKE, TRYING TO GET HIM LOOSE, BUT SPIKE WAS HANGING ON FOR DEAR LIFE! THEY FELL TO THE GROUND AND THE BEAR'S ROAR WAS NOW GARGLED, AS HE CONTINUED PAWING AND PULLING AT SPIKE.

SPIKE'S GROWL WAS FEROCIOUS AND HIS ATTACK HAD BEEN GRUESOME, BUT HE WAS NOW LOSING HIS HOLD. THE BEAR STOOD ON ITS BACK LEGS AND PULLED SPIKE LOOSE FROM ITS THROAT, THEN THREW HIM TO THE GROUND! HAVING HAD ALL OF SPIKE IT WANTED, IT DROPPED DOWN ON ALL FOURS AND HEADED TOWARD THE CREEK, BUT AFTER GOING ONLY A FEW FEET, IT FELL TO THE GROUND WITH A THUD! IT LAY THERE, KICKING AND CLAWING, TRYING TO GET UP.

AFTER SEVERAL MINUTES, THE BEAR GOT TO ITS FEET, BUT WAS WOBBLING AS IT TRIED TO RUN. IT FELL AGAIN, AND THIS TIME, IT LAY THERE, NOT MOV-ING.

BY NOW, SALLY AND TOM WERE BACK IN THE HOUSE WITH THE DOORS LOCKED, WATCHING THROUGH THE WINDOW. SUDDENLY, SALLY STARTED HAVING PAINS; SHE WAS GOING INTO LABOR, AND THE BABY WASN'T DUE FOR ANOTHER TWO MONTHS!

WE HAD HEARD THE SCREAMS AND KNEW THEY WERE COMING FROM MY PLACE, AND WE WERE RUNNING AS FAST AS WE COULD! WHEN WE BROKE INTO THE CLEAR-ING JUST SOUTH OF THE HOUSE, WE SAW NOTHING.

THERE WERE NO SOUNDS AT ALL. THEN THERE WAS A
SCREAM! IT WAS COMING FROM THE HOUSE, AND I JUST
KNEW THE BEAR WAS INSIDE!

GEORGE AND I RACED FOR THE HOUSE! JUST
BEFORE WE GOT TO THE PORCH, GEORGE POINTED TOWARD
THE CREEK AND HOLLERED, "LOOK!" I LOOKED AND SAW
SPIKE AND THE BEAR. THEY WERE LYING ON THE
GROUND A FEW YARDS APART.

WHEN WE RAN INTO THE HOUSE, SALLY WAS IN
LABOR AND THE PAINS WERE CONSTANT. BONNIE SAID,
"THANK GOODNESS YOU'RE HERE! SALLY'S HAVING THE
BABY RIGHT NOW!"

I RAN OUTSIDE AND SAID, "SOMEONE GO FOR
THE DOCTOR; SALLY'S IN LABOR. USE THE SCHOOL
BELL TO SIGNAL TROUBLE, THEN GIVE HIM THE MESSAGE.
AND TELL HIM TO HURRY!"

I WENT BACK INTO THE HOUSE AND TOLD SALLY
THAT I'D SENT FOR THE DOCTOR. SHE SAID, "DAVE,
GO CHECK ON SPIKE."

WHEN I GOT OUTSIDE, EVERYONE WAS GATHERED
AROUND THE BEAR. HIS THROAT HAD BEEN RIPPED OPEN
AND HIS JUGGLER VEIN SEVERED. THE BEAR HAD BLED
TO DEATH.

I HURRIED OVER TO SPIKE. HE HAD BEEN
RIPPED AND CLAWED ALL OVER, BUT HE WAS STILL
BREATHING. I COULDN'T SEE HOW HE COULD STILL BE
ALIVE WITH HIS BODY TORN TO SHREDS LIKE THAT.
GEORGE AND I CARRIED HIM TO THE HOUSE. BONNIE
COVERED THE KITCHEN TABLE WITH A QUILT, AND WE
LAID HIM ON IT AND COVERED HIM UP. THERE WAS

NOTHING WE COULD DO NOW BUT WAIT FOR THE DOCTOR TO SHOW UP.

I WENT OUTSIDE AND SAW THAT THE MEN WERE GETTING READY TO SKIN THE BEAR. GEORGE STOPPED THEM, SAYING, "WAIT! LET'S TAKE THE BEAR TO THE CANNERY AND GET IT WEIGHED." THE OTHERS AGREED, SO GEORGE HARNESSED MY TEAM AND HITCHED THEM TO THE WAGON.

IT TOOK EVERYONE THERE TO PICK UP THE BEAR AND PUT HIM ON THE WAGON. WE GUESSED HIS WEIGHT AT NEAR EIGHT HUNDRED POUNDS.

WE COULD HEAR THE SCHOOL BELL RINGING IN THE DISTANCE AND FIGURED THE DOCTOR WOULD BE GETTING THE WORD ANY TIME NOW.

GEORGE AND THE MEN HEADED FOR THE CANNERY WITH THE BEAR, AND I WENT INSIDE TO BE WITH SALLY. I SAT ON THE EDGE OF THE BED AND HELD HER HAND AND SAID, "SALLY, I JUST HEARD THE SCHOOL BELL RINGING, SO THE DOCTOR IS PROBABLY ON HIS WAY."

SHE ASKED, "WHAT ABOUT SPIKE? IS HE GOING TO BE ALL RIGHT?" THEN HER FACE TURNED WHITE, AND SHE ASKED, "IS SPIKE DEAD?"

I SAID, "NO, HE'S HURT BAD, BUT HE'S ALIVE."

ABOUT AN HOUR HAD PASSED WHEN GEORGE WALKED IN. HE SAID, "WELL, THE BEAR WEIGHED EIGHT HUNDRED AND EIGHTY POUNDS! ALL THE MEN AGREE THAT IT'S THE BIGGEST BLACK BEAR THAT ANYONE HAS EVER SEEN AROUND HERE."

Bonnie came over to us and said, "Dave, why don't you and George wait outside." So we went outside and sat on the porch.

The doctor finally showed up and hurried to the bedroom where Sally was. George and I checked on Spike. He was whining low and his breathing was still regular. He was tough and had a strong will to live.

The doctor had been in the room with Sally for a good thirty minutes. When he came into the kitchen he was smiling, and that made me feel good. He said, "Well, Dave, you and Sally have a baby girl."

I said, "Doc, why didn't we hear her cry?"

He said, "Not all babies cry when they're born; some just gasp for air and start breathing on their own. From every indication, she'll be fine."

I said, "Doc, Spike killed the bear, but he's hurt real bad. Can you do something for him?"

He said, "I'll do all I can." He went over to the table and removed the quilt from Spike. A lump came to my throat and tears fell from my eyes as I looked down and saw that he wasn't breathing. Spike was dead ...

"An animal's instinct to protect the ones it loves is stronger than its instinct to survive."

Dave Sargent